CRACKER BLING

Nineteen-year-old Hootie has been in trouble all his life. An outsider, his father was Crow Indian; his mother is black; but Hootie is neither black, nor white, nor Latino, nor Asian. When he meets 'Bubba' Yablonsky, the biggest white man he's ever seen, at a subway station in Harlem, he knows something's up. Then Bubba opens fire at an innocent rat before offering Hootie money and a place to live. But what's the catch? And what else – who else – has Bubba shot?

CRACKER BLING

Stephen Solomita

Severn House Large Print
London & New York

This first large print edition published 2010
in Great Britain and the USA by
SEVERN HOUSE PUBLISHERS LTD of
9-15 High Street, Sutton, Surrey, SM1 1DF.
First world regular print edition published 2008 by
Severn House Publishers Ltd., London and New York.

British Library Cataloguing in Publication Data

Solomita, Stephen.
  Cracker bling.
  1. Racially mixed people--Fiction. 2. Burglars--Fiction.
  3. Problem youth--Fiction. 4. Detectives--New York
  (State)--New York--Fiction. 5. Murder--Investigation--
  New York (State)--New York--Fiction. 6. New York (N.Y.)--
  Fiction. 7. Detective and mystery stories. 8. Large type
  books.
  I. Title
  813.5'4-dc22

  ISBN-13: 978-0-7278-7861-8

Printed and bound in Great Britain by
MPG Books Ltd, Bodmin, Cornwall.

cracker 95 n. an offensive term employed by African–Americans to disparage Caucasians

bling 95 n. US informal (formerly **bling-bling**) the outward manifestations of material success

— ORIGIN 1990s: perhaps imitative of light reflecting off jewelry

ONE

The descent is nothing, a single flight of stairs leading from the street into the subway station at 145th Street and Broadway. How many times has Hootie, at age nineteen, tripped down these stairs? Hundreds, definitely – maybe thousands. It's New York City, it's July and this is West Harlem, land of the forlorn and forgotten, categories in which Hootie definitely includes himself. Still, Hootie feels as if he's descending into hell itself. The heat rises up to greet him, wet as a predator's tongue, the stench, too, of piss and mildew and a hundred years of steel dust and axle grease. The atmosphere is sharp enough to sting his eyes, sour enough to make him force the air he reluctantly breathes through clenched teeth. Beneath the worn soles of his low-end Nikes, the steps are greasy, while the rail beneath his hand is pocked with rust and the grimy wall tiles are slick with condensed humidity.

Hootie has been using the system long enough to know that most of the 1 Line's downtown stations, where the white people live, where the tourists congregate, have been refurbished. The tiles gleam, white as snow, and colorful mosaics brighten the walls. Not so uptown. No, no, not at all. Up here, it's strictly Black to the back. You don't like the filth, close your eyes. You don't like the stink, don't breathe.

Hootie listens to the fading roar of a 1 Train heading south into Manhattan, the train he would have caught if he'd come down the stairs only a few seconds before. Trains run infrequently in the early morning hours and the wait for the next one is sure to be long. But Hootie has nowhere to go. At nineteen years old, a week out of Rikers Island Correctional Facility, he's now also officially homeless, his sainted mom having kicked him out of her apartment twenty minutes before. Or better put, his mom's fool of a husband, a tight-ass Jamaican named Archie Couch, having kicked him out.

'Yo boy, ya don't be livin' here no more. Ya

8

bring only harm to the household.'

Hootie had wanted to slap the pompous bastard. He'd wanted to knock Archie on his tight ass. And Hootie would have, too, without thinking twice, if probation hadn't been a condition of his release. Which brings up another problem. What's gonna happen when his probation officer makes a home visit, an eventuality sure to occur within the next couple of weeks? Bad enough he doesn't have a job. Now he doesn't have a home either. Now he's really and truly and absolutely fucked.

Hootie takes a moment to scan the station, including the stairs behind him. Looking for the Man, a reflex that comes to him as naturally as it comes to anybody raised in Harlem, a reflex honed to a razor's edge in the Otis Bantum Correctional Center on Rikers Island. Life in Otis Bantum was about watching your back at all times. Still is, for that matter, a point he definitely needs to consider because it's growing more and more likely that he'll be returning in the near future.

But there are no cops in sight, not at the moment, no human beings of any kind except for a clerk snoring away in her bullet-proof token booth.

Hootie jumps the turnstile and finds a seat on a long wooden bench. He glances to his left, along the length of the platform and into the tunnel. He was wrong about it just being him and the clerk in the station. There's a drunk passed out at the far the end of the platform. A plume of urine fans out from his crotch.

Hootie pinches his nostrils in a vain attempt to shut out the stink, then settles back. He's a tall boy, not quite a man, with a wiry build toned in an Otis Bantum weight room. His hair is coarse, thick and dark. Cut by a Rikers Island barber, it grips the side of his head, tight as a skullcap. Hootie's decided to let his hair grow out and that's what set his mother off. Hootie's dad was a full-blooded Crow Indian who died when Hootie was twelve. Hootie's mother, Corlie Couch, is a black woman and very much alive. She wants Hootie to embrace his black identity, but Hootie's not buying. Neither black, nor white, nor Latino, nor Asian, he's been an outsider all his life. In grammar school, the bullies among his schoolmates called him 'What-Is-It?'

Almost from his first day at Otis Bantum,

when he wasn't actively engaged in the fine art of survival, Hootie considered some aspect of his identity. Not his race, not at first. Hootie was labeled a criminal, officially, on the day he pled guilty to three downtown burglaries. And from that day forward, for the next nine months, morning, noon and night, he lived in a fifty-bed dormitory with other labeled criminals. Otis Bantum housed only post-conviction inmates. It was a prison, not a jail.

But that didn't make Hootie a criminal, not to Hootie's way of thinking. The Corrections Officers called him 'mutt' and 'piece of shit' and 'nigger'. They controlled where he went and what he did. But they couldn't control his mind, no more than the judge who sentenced him, Judge Irene Bolardi, whose voice had rung with contempt.

'You have no excuse, Mr. Hootier. You have a mother and father who work, and your sister's an attorney. There was always food on the table and a roof over your head. You have ability, too, and talent – as your school records amply demonstrate. No, Mr. Hootier, you had all the advantages, but you chose to become a criminal. Now you have to pay the price.'

Hootie had just stood there with his head down. Trying not to smile. He was OK with his lawyer's advice – show remorse – but he was thinking, Yeah, I got no excuse. Not like them other niggers. Not like them abused niggers, them retarded niggers, them neglected niggers.

Bolardi had gone on for a few minutes, then asked Hootie if he had anything to say. Hootie had nodded before reciting a little speech his lawyer had urged him to memorize.

'I know I messed up my family. I know I let them down. I made a lot of mistakes, your Honor, and I'm hopin' you'll give me another chance to make it up to them.'

All bullshit, every word, because his sentence had been determined in advance and probation was off the table. Bolardi was gonna sentence him to a year, to be served on Rikers Island. If he was a reasonably good boy, he might be released in as little as nine months. And that was the sole reason for his apology. If he didn't show remorse at time of sentencing, the parole board would penalize him on the back end.

Seven months into his bid, Hootie finally

12

decided that he was only a criminal if he labeled himself a criminal. Otherwise ... Hootie wasn't sure about the otherwise, but his thoughts inevitably led him to ask a different question. Though he hung with the brothers as a matter of necessity, he could not make himself believe that he was any more Black than he was Indian. Black was a label he'd been given. It was not the face he confronted in the mirror every morning when he shaved. Hootie had his mother's marble-round eyes, but every other feature was inherited from his father: the flat brow, the aquiline nose, the hollow cheeks, the narrow mouth. And his pale copper skin was so light that cops had to ask him his race.

Hell, his father's heritage was embedded in Hootie's very name: Judson Two-Bears Hootier, Jr.

Earlier, Hootie had made a clumsy attempt to explain all of this to his mother. They were in the living room, Hootie, his mom and Archie the asshole, watching *The Original Kings of Comedy*.

'I think I'm gonna let my hair grow out, maybe wear it down to my shoulders. Like my father used to.'

His mom had asked, her voice already edging up, 'Why you wanna go there?'

'I want to find out who I am.'

'What, black isn't good enough for you?'

'It ain't just about black.'

'Uh-oh, here comes a story.'

This familiar complaint – that Hootie makes it up as he goes along – is a gambit Hootie ignores. 'It's about criminal and minority and dumb and a hundred more labels been put on me. I gotta peel up the labels, see what's underneath. I don't, I'll never get out from under.'

'If you wanna get out from under, find a damn job.'

Another gambit ignored. 'I had a father, too,' Hootie insisted.

But his mom wasn't listening and the conversation heated up, as it always did, as it always had, until Hootie finally blew his cool.

'You buyin' into the white man's game. And why? 'Cause a hundred years ago some cracker said that one drop taints the whole man? And look at you anyway, light as you are. You think your green eyes came out of Africa?'

★ ★ ★

14

Hootie laughs to himself, laughs despite his predicament. Questioning his mother's identity was like asking a white prison guard why his momma sucks black cock. Hootie was out the door so fast he caught a wind burn.

The turnstile to Hootie's right flips over with a sharp *ka-chunk*. Without moving his head so much as a millimeter, Hootie scopes out the new arrival, a short, moon-faced Latino with a banana for a nose. The man wears baggy jeans and a T-shirt embroidered with a rhinestone skull. He glances at Hootie, then drifts off in the opposite direction.

Hootie runs the back of his hand over the sweat that coats his forehead, then lays his hand in his lap. If possible, the stench is becoming even more nauseating. It reminds him of the six days and nights he spent in solitary confinement at Otis Bantum. The toilet had backed up on day two and the COs had predictably ignored his complaints. By the time they cut him loose on the seventh morning, the floor was covered with sewage.

The turnstile spins twice more and a pair of Latinas emerge. Maybe thirteen or fourteen years old, the Latinas are wearing skin-tight Baby Phat jeans and tank-tops revealing enough to make Hootie shift in his seat. A man follows. He's not young, but his manner is fiercely protective. A father, or maybe an uncle, yanking the girls out of a party somewhere.

A northbound train rips into the station, the thrum of its engines and screech of its brakes loud enough to drown thought. The train pushes enough air forward to create a momentary breeze that cools the sweat on Hootie's face and neck. He looks in the other direction for a southbound train, a train sure to be air-conditioned. No such luck. Across the track, the air brakes on the northbound train release with a collective hiss and the train moves on, revealing a few stragglers drifting along platform. The last man out is singing in Spanish and Hootie wonders if he's one of the city's many street psychos or merely drunk. Before he can decide, the turnstile flips again. This time, the figure that emerges, a white man in his late twenties, captures Hootie's full attention. This is the biggest white man Hootie has ever seen – big like Shack, like an interior lineman – wearing a red Hawaiian shirt large enough to be a tablecloth and cargo shorts that drop below his knees. His head is enormous, but his features are small and regular. 'Baby-faced' is the description that pops into Hootie's mind, until he looks into the man's flint-gray eyes.

Turning away, Hootie flashes back to a conversation he had with a middle-aged con named Eli Scannon. Scannon was a jail-house philosopher who became Hootie's mentor at Otis Bantum.

'Mostly,' Eli told him one day, 'the white man believes all that bullshit he been sellin' for the last hundred years. About the black man's so-called appetite for violence. And mostly the white man is afraid of the black man. But there are some white men out there you don't wanna mess with, especially if he's wearin' a uniform. This is a lesson the black man tends to learn the hard way.'

Well, the man now sitting at the other end of the bench isn't wearing a uniform. But that doesn't mean he's not a cop. Hootie's thinking maybe it's time to move on. He looks into the tunnel again. No help from that quarter.

'Yo, you want a hit?'

Hootie smells the weed before he sees it, a

fat joint extended between fingers long enough to enclose his entire face. Somebody in Hootie's head, his conscience, his guardian angel, screams, *Noooooooooooo* ... But Hootie accepts the joint even before the echo dies away. He is so fucked up and he so needs to get high. He needs to have one thing in his life that isn't about hopeless and helpless.

After a second hit, Hootie's mellow enough to refuse a third. He watches the man carefully stub the joint out and slide the roach into his shirt pocket. For a moment, as the man lifts his arm, Hootie's marijuana-addled attention is drawn to the flock of green and gold parrots that encircle the man's shirt. High being high, after all, he's thinking they might fly away.

'Conrad Yablonsky. People call me Bubba.'

Hootie stares at the hand extended in his direction, then says, 'Judson Two-Bears Hootier. But Hootie'll be good enough.'

Bubba squeezes gently, but his power is evident, a message sent and received. Again, Hootie tells himself to get off his ass, move away. And he would if he had somewhere to go. As it is, he settles on the bench and

18

creates a mental list of friends and acquaintances. Hootie wants to avoid the shelter system if at all possible, and not just because the shelters are almost as dangerous as the housing units on Otis Bantum. Talk about hopeless and helpless. Talk about a future without horizons.

But his other options aren't much better. Yeah, there are people out there who'll lend him a piece of floor to sleep on. The same people he hung with before he was sentenced, his partners in crime. Another road he does not want to go down.

'Hootie, check this out, man.'

Hootie glances at Bubba, then detects movement on the other side of the station, an enormous rat, big even by New York standards, coming from the end of the platform furthest from the station's entrance. The rat dashes forward, running hunchbacked, tail as thick as a bullwhip, only to stop suddenly, nose raised and twitching.

Hootie watches the animal repeat the process several times, then suddenly grins. 'Dinner,' he announces.

Bubba nods once, then raises the tail of his Hawaiian shirt and slides an automatic pistol from beneath his waistband. He winks at Hootie and says, 'I hate rats,' before firing off a barrage of shots that come too fast to be counted.

Hootie is stunned, as if some higher power has grabbed hold of his brain, squeezing for all it's worth. His mouth drops open, even as every other muscle in his body goes rigid. He can't believe what he's seeing. There are three rows of steel columns separating Bubba from his target and the far wall is tiled. Hootie doesn't know which of these surfaces is being hit by the fusillade, but ricochets are flying in all directions. It's like an old western, where the good guy and the bad guy are shooting it out on some rocky hillside. Ka-blam, ka-blam. Ping, zing. Passengers on both sides of the platforms are running for the only exit, pushing through the turnstiles, galloping up the stairs to the street. A woman begins to scream and Hootie wonders if she's been hit. When he turns his head to look, she's in an all-out sprint.

'Enough bullshit.'

Bubba rises to his feet and takes careful aim, holding the gun in two massive hands, sighting along the barrel, finally squeezing off a last shot. Hit dead center, the rat literally explodes, its various parts – bone, blood and viscera – splattering against the wall. A few seconds later, as a southbound train pulls into the station, Bubba stoops to retrieve the shell casings scattered to the right of the bench, all except the one lodged between the bench and the tiled wall.

'Our carriage awaits,' he tells Hootie.

TWO

Within seconds, Hootie's dumbfounded shock is replaced by anger. Young as he is, Hootie's no punk. Never mind the fact that Bubba has to bend over to enter the train, or that his head brushes the top of the car. Never mind the fact that Bubba's packing serious heat. There are times when you have to stand up for yourself, no matter what the odds.

Hootie balls his right hand into a fist and says, 'Listen up. I'm a week out of Rikers and I'm on probation. If I get violated because of your asshole move, I swear to God I'll cap your dumb ass. I don't care if it takes me the rest of my fucking life.'

Bubba looks down at Hootie and smiles, which only pisses Hootie off all the more. 'Hey, take it easy. I'm just a month out of the joint. I'm on parole, myself.'

'The only thing you're out of is your

fuckin' mind.'

Hootie listens to the sound of his own voice. He's still high, of course, and he feels as though he's eavesdropping on someone else's conversation. Even his anger seems remote. But then Bubba nods thoughtfully and it's obvious that he's giving Hootie's complaint a hearing.

'Ya know, I was up in Clinton for two years before they shipped me to Green Haven. Talk about a tough joint? You get out of line, the COs beat you with axe handles.'

'Didn't I just—?'

'I heard you, Hootie. But just let me say what I have to say.' Bubba hesitates long enough to lay a massive hand on Hootie's shoulder. 'In the institution, the Man's only got one game and that's to break your spirit. You hear what I'm sayin'? And you really can't blame the COs. With rehabilitation off the table, the only way to control the population is to break the inmates, physically and psychologically. And it's not just the beatings, or gettin' thrown in solitary. It's about the strip searches. It's about trashing your cell during shakedowns. It's about screws who call you "piece of shit", or "asshole", or "scumbag". It's about ten thousand other humiliations designed for only one purpose, to break your spirit, so that when they finally cut your loose, you're not good for anything more than shakin' a cup. "Spare change, sir? Spare a quarter?" '

The speech slows Hootie down precisely because the ideas Bubba tosses out so closely parallel his own. What do you do when the whole world's beating you down? How do you make your way? Hootie doesn't have many answers, but he's certain that killing rats on subway platforms is a losing strategy.

Hootie takes a minute to check his surroundings. Despite the hour, there are passengers scattered throughout the car, the usual mix of races and nationalities. At the far end, three Latino knuckleheads glare into space. Two wear black hoodies pulled over their heads. The other wears a T-shirt that reaches his knees. Badasses or wannabes? Hootie's not sure.

'Lemme ask you this...' Hootie finally says.
'Shoot.'
'No, don't shoot. Leave the piece where it is. Because if committing suicide is the only way to keep my spirit alive, I'm ready to get on my knees and start sucking cock.'

Bubba's laugh fills the train, drawing the attention of the other passengers, including the three assholes at the far end of the car. Hootie watches them stir, eyes swinging to Bubba as they make a careful assessment. Bubba, on the other hand, pays no attention. It's as if they're alone.

'Stick with me awhile,' he says when Hootie finally calms down. 'Let's talk.'

They ride in silence, down to Fourteenth Street where they catch a cross-town L to First Avenue. Hootie takes a deep breath when they finally reach the street. The temperature has fallen to eighty degrees and the humid air seems pristine compared to the air in the station. As Bubba leads the way to a narrow promenade that runs between the East River and FDR Drive, Hootie opens up, describing a history that includes his homeless state and the reasons for it.

'See, that's just what I mean,' Bubba says when Hootie grinds to halt. 'Your mom? Your stepfather? They want to throw you down, put their feet on the back of your head. They want you to show submission, like a dog. All that crap about your identity?

That's an excuse, Hootie. Even if you memorized every speech Martin Luther King ever made, they'd find a reason to make you crawl. And the funny part is they don't even know they're doin' it. They think they love you.'

The early morning is overcast and the air smells of fish. Hootie can taste the salt on his tongue. To his left, the river is flat and black, a mirror that returns the city's lights as if rejecting a gift. To his right, the few cars on FDR Drive whip past at high speed, here and gone. Bubba looks around, then yanks the automatic from beneath his shirt.

'Two hundred dollars. That's what I paid for the piece.' Bubba hesitates, but when Hootie doesn't respond, he shrugs his shoulders. 'From the half-court line,' he announces, before scaling the gun out over the water. The weapon describes a long arc, spinning like a Frisbee, before dropping into the river some thirty yards away. A moment later, a handful of shell casings follow.

'You get caught with a handgun,' Bubba declares, 'it's three and a half years, mandatory.'

Without further explanation, Bubba leads

Hootie south, toward the Tenth Street overpass. 'You need a place to stay, you could bunk with me for a couple of days. I got room.'

And what can Hootie say to that? I'd rather spend the night on the street? Hootie watches the elongated shadows in front of him, his alongside Bubba's. He's thinking he looks like a kid walking beside his father. Thinking, not for the first time, that he's somehow climbed the beanstalk.

'Yeah, that'd be good.'

'And there's somebody I want you to meet.'

Hootie doesn't respond. He's pretty certain that he's being played, that Bubba's trying to sell him something. But if listening to Bubba's sales pitch is the price of a room, it's a price Hootie's willing to pay, especially now that Bubba's gun is in the river. They recross FDR Drive at Tenth Street, walking west through the Lillian Wald Houses, a low-income project that runs for blocks in either direction. Hootie's visited the projects that dot West Harlem many times and the ground isn't unfamiliar. Still, his brain jumps to full alert when a black man steps out of the shadows and walks directly toward them.

'Yo, Bubba, s'up?'

'Nothin' to it.' Bubba offers a forearm which the man dutifully bumps.

'You gonna win tomorrow?'

'The kid they got at center, he's too small. I can handle him.'

'But I'm askin' if you gonna win.'

'I'm gonna have a good game. Beyond that, I got nothin' to say.'

'I hear ya.'

The man walks back into the shadows without so much as glancing at Hootie. Bubba watches him for a moment before continuing on to Avenue D. They're on the Lower East Side of Manhattan, in an area gentrifiers call Alphabet City.

'I play in a basketball league,' Bubba explains, 'twice a week. Asshole drug dealers sponsor the teams and bet on the games. There's even a point spread. But the thing is, this league, half the players are ex-cons like me. So it ain't a question of whether points are being shaved, but only who's shaving them.'

Hootie finally puts the pieces together. He was ten or eleven, he can't remember exactly, but the story was big news for months. The starting forward at St. John's, a white kid on full scholarship, got into a fight with a teammate, a fight the teammate did not survive. Basketball had more or less defined Hootie's world back in the day, and Hootie distinctly remembers the public outcry when the killer was allowed to plea bargain the original murder charge down to manslaughter.

'You're that dude from St. John's.'

'No, Hootie, I'm not that *dude*. I'm that power forward who was a dead lock to go in the first round of the NBA draft. That power forward who was lookin' at a minimum two million dollar signing bonus.'

Bubba leads Hootie across Avenue D and halfway up the block before coming to a halt. They're standing beneath a tree, a sycamore, with the light from a street lamp bleeding through the leaves. The light is falling across Bubba's head and shoulders like a spotlight and it occurs to Hootie that his companion deliberately chose the setting.

'See, it wasn't like they said, what they wrote about. I mean, the jerk got in my face one too many times and I gave him a beat down. I admit that. And I admit that I beat him bad, alright? But the fact is that he was in the emergency room fifteen minutes after I got off him and the docs said he was OK. You hear me, right? The docs examined him, took his blood, gave him a CT scan, and sent the poor bastard home. Six hours later, he's dead from internal bleeding, which naturally is my fault. I tell ya, Hootie, if I wasn't playin' big-time ball, I wouldn't have gotten more than a year. I mean, it's not like the asshole wasn't fightin' back. But every judge is a law-and-order judge when the media's lookin' over his shoulder. Same for the DA. They don't wanna look soft on crime, so they make an example.'

'And the example was you.'

'Take it to the bank.'

Hootie looks Bubba right in the eye. Time to take a stand. 'If you were innocent, why did you plead guilty?'

'Simple, they were gonna charge me with murder unless I took the plea and my lawyer wouldn't guarantee an acquittal. Ten years is a long time – I oughta know – but it's a lot less than twenty-five to life.'

They continue west, to Avenue A. As they

wait for the light, a police cruiser drifts by, slowing as it comes alongside them. The two cops inside fix them with a hard stare, a stare that challenges even as it dismisses them. Hootie absorbs the stare without flinching, but doesn't begin to relax until the cops move on. This is something else he'll never shake, this reaction to cops. He might cover the tension, might not show it on the outside, but inside he'll always feel a mix of rage and fear, the emotions curling around each other like mating snakes.

'See there,' Bubba says as they cross the street. 'Those cops, they'll remember.'

'Remember what?'

'Remember me, Hootie. And that's my whole problem. Big as I am, nobody forgets me. I'm conspicuous wherever I go. Now you, you're just the opposite. If those cops try to describe you an hour from now, they won't even know what to call you. White, black, Hispanic, even Asian or Muslim. You could be anything.'

They cross First Avenue before Bubba pulls to a halt in front of a five-story brick town-house. The townhouse is in good repair, the brick clean enough to have been freshly laid.

There's a fan window above a lacquered oak door and window boxes on the third floor that bear impatiens, begonias and a lime-green ivy, white at the borders, that trails along the brick.

'Home sweet home, at least temporarily,' Bubba says. 'I'm house-sitting for the owners. They're in Morocco. Which means we have to be quiet and keep the place neat. The neighbors are real assholes, which naturally follows from the fact that they have money.' Bubba winks. 'Now me, I can't wait to have money. Then I can be an asshole, too.'

Bubba climbs the stoop, two steps at a time, and shoves a key in the door lock. He leads Hootie up three flights of winding stairs, past a series of vintage city photographs, to an apartment door. With a flourish, he unlocks the door, leans inside and calls, softly, 'You decent?'

A girl's voice answers. 'We have company?'

'That we do.' Bubba shoves the door open to reveal a young, very blonde girl. He steps inside, Hootie following, then closes the door and locks both locks. Finally, he gestures to Hootie and says, 'This is Two-Bears Hootier, better known as Hootie. Hootie, this is Amelia Cincone. She has a nickname, too, but before I tell you what it is, try to guess Amelia's age.'

Hootie figures the girl in front of him can't be more than nine or ten. Tall for her age, maybe, but she has neither breasts nor hips. Growing up, Hootie watched his older sister mature into a woman, so he believes himself familiar with the process. Still, there has to be a point here, otherwise Bubba wouldn't have raised the question a few seconds after they walked through the door.

'Nine?' Hootie guesses.

'Add ten years.' Bubba's grinning. 'Show him,' he tells Amelia.

Amelia hesitates just long enough for Hootie to read her age in her eyes. There's no child in those blue eyes. Not even close. He watches her rummage through her purse for a moment, then turn to offer him a pair of documents. The first is a driver's license bearing her photograph, the second a birth certificate. Both confirm her age.

'Kallmann syndrome,' she tells Hootie. 'For reasons unknown, but probably having to do with a genetic mutation, my hypothalamus doesn't produce sex hormones, so my body didn't mature.' She looks down, bats her eyelashes, finally curtsies. 'I'm Patricia Pan,' she tells Hootie. 'I'm a freak.'

Bubba takes out a roll of bills, a thick roll. 'Seed money,' he explains passing it to Amelia. He lays an arm around Amelia's shoulder while she thumbs through the roll, greedy as a child in a toy store. 'Alright, now, we've done the show. It's time for the tell. Like I already said, Amelia's has a nickname. Can you guess what it is?'

Hootie shakes his head. 'Not a clue.'

'Meal ticket.'

Later, Hootie's sitting on the edge of a platform bed in a smallish bedroom while he strips off his shoes, socks and pants. He's never been fond of modern furniture and the decor throughout the apartment, which covers the entire floor, is all glass, chrome and abstract paintings, with the occasional pop art canvas thrown in for contrast. But like it or not, the entire apartment screams money, leaving Hootie to wonder how Bubba came to be living here. The foam mattress is cradling his ass like the hand of a lover.

Hootie folds his clothes and lays them across a wicker side chair with a pink cushion on the seat, another habit learned in prison where he pressed his Rikers Island jumpsuit by laying it beneath his mattress while he slept. He turns off the bedside lamp and drops his head to a stack of pillows. He, Bubba and Amelia had shared a nightcap, some kind of bourbon from a jug, then gone off to separate bedrooms. Amelia and Bubba were business partners, not lovers. This pleased Hootie – nineteen or not, the scene was too perverted for his tastes. But it left him restless, too. Bubba was slowly pulling him in, just as the foam mattress was curling around his body. Right now, this minute, if Bubba hadn't come along, he'd be sleeping on a subway train, or walking the streets, waiting for sunrise and a quick nap on a park bench. Instead, he's pulling up a comforter to ward off the chill of the air conditioner, a comforter nearly as soft as the sheets and the pillowcases, which are as soft as satin. And how do you say no to that? Given the alternatives?

Hootie's last thoughts are of his prison mentor, Eli Scannon. Eli was a small man who'd survived many years in New York's worst prisons. He had tiny eyes that he squeezed down when he was excited, so that he looked at you through narrow slits. And his hands were always moving, though the rest of his body remained still.

'When the heat comes down,' he told Hootie, 'the white man will always betray the black man. And it don't matter how close they are, don't matter if they was asshole buddies. When the shit hits the fan, it's the black man's face gonna be in front of the blades. Now the thing about the white man is that he can't admit it, not even to himself. No, the white man will sell the black man's ass down the river, then pronounce himself righteous. Myself, I prefer the other kind of white man, the one who wanna see niggers hangin' from every tree. I feel safer with him.'

THREE

Detective Peter Chigorin, universally called the Russian by his peers, can't believe what he's seeing. The 1 Line shut down in both directions at 145th Street. Enough crime-scene tape to decorate the Christmas tree at Rockefeller Center. A dozen crime-scene cops swarming over both platforms. A knot of uniformed officers, including a lieutenant, drinking coffee by the token booth. A pair of detectives huddled over a drunk who falls on his face whenever he tries to stand up.

And for what? For a dead rat? Because that's the only victim on the Russian's immediate horizon: what's left of a dead rat surrounded by a forest of yellow tape.

The Russian strolls down to the end of the platform and removes what appears to be a thick, leather notebook from his pocket. The notebook is actually a flask with enough vodka at the bottom for a final chug. With his back to the assembled cops, Chigorin drains the flask, thinking, This is gonna be a short visit.

Detective Chigorin, of the prestigious Homicide Division, is not here to investigate a shooting in which no human being was injured. He's investigating the murder of a drug dealer on Hamilton Place, two blocks away. As the murder occurred minutes before the rat shooting, the Russian naturally needs to know if the two incidents are related. This should not be a big deal. A single shell casing was recovered on the subway platform and a pair of shell casings was recovered at the scene of the murder. They'll match or they won't.

Officially, the rat case belongs to the two detectives at the other end of the platform, Budlow and O'Malley. They're questioning the drunk, who's now squatting. Chigorin can smell the drunk from where he stands, a stench that will not abate as he draws closer to its source. Nevertheless, he walks the length of the platform.

'Hey, Chigorin, what happened to the Arab?' Budlow asks. The Arab is Ahmad Mansouri, Chigorin's partner.

'Sciatica.'

'Again? How long does he expect to get away with this sciatica bullshit? Every time I turn around he's gettin' paid to sit on his ass.' Budlow is small and overweight. His complexion is florid to begin with, but when he becomes indignant, as he is now, the color along his cheekbones approaches the red of a fire engine.

'Fucked if I know,' Chigorin responds agreeably. 'Anyway, I got a homicide took place a couple of blocks away. Two shots, one to the back, one to the head. The woman who called in the shooting claims she dialed nine-one-one right away. That was at three twenty-five.'

Budlow chews this over for a moment, then says, 'Look, you wanna fold this shooting into your case, it's fine by me.'

Budlow's partner, Ralph O'Malley, agrees the motion. The Chinese takeout on his desk is growing colder by the minute. 'No problem here if you wanna take over,' he says.

In fact, the Russian has no desire to take the case. He's sweating like a pig and wants only to be out on the street where he can breathe. But the thing about the Russian, a fault he's reproached himself for maybe ten thousand times, is that he has a conscience about taking the Man's pay and doing the Man's job. Which is really amazing in that he's fucked up the rest of his life entirely.

'So, what have you got?' he asks.

'A surveillance tape from the camera near the booth and one nine millimeter shell casing.' Budlow gestures to the drunk. 'And Homer. Homer claims he was asleep when the shooting went down. Claims he didn't wake up until we arrived.'

'What about the token clerk?'

'Also asleep when the shots were fired. She says when she opened her eyes, people were flyin' out of the station. She called it in, by the way, at three thirty-seven.'

No fools, Budlow and O'Malley only hang around long enough to change the information on the evidence bags containing the surveillance tapes and the cartridge casing. That done, they're up the stairs nearly as fast as the passengers fleeing Bubba's fusillade. The Russian doesn't stick around all that long, either. He quizzes the first cops on the scene, but they have nothing to add. The station was empty when they got here.

40

Except for Homer, the only game in town.

The Russian grabs Homer by the collar and hauls him down the platform. When Homer falls and starts to choke, the Russian keeps on going, though he carefully skirts a puddle of urine. He doesn't stop until they reach the steps at the end of the platform, the ones that lead into the tunnel.

'What the fuck, what the fuck? Where are we goin'?'

'I'm takin' you into the tunnel so I can beat the shit out of you.'

'Oh, man, why you wanna do me like that?'

'Because you're disrespectin' me.'

'How ah'm disrespectin' you?'

'Eight gunshots? In a subway station? You know how loud a gunshot is down here? Loud enough to wake the fuckin' dead, that's how loud. But here you come along asking me to believe that you slept right through the gunshots but conveniently woke up when the cops arrived. That's disrespectful.'

Homer's shaking his head as fast as he can. The Russian can almost see the man's brain rattling inside his skull. As he can see the truth in the man's jaundiced eyes.

41

Homer was, indeed, asleep, which is all Chigorin wants to know.

'Reason I woke up,' Homer explains to the Russian's retreating back, 'is that fat cop kicked me right in the ass. My ass is still hurtin'.'

One more stop and I'm outta here, Chigorin thinks as he makes his way to Sergeant Ernie Boyle of the Crime Scene Unit. Boyle and Chigorin have disliked each other for many years.

'I want you to collect the rat,' Chigorin says.

'Twice in one night? Why me, Lord?'

The Russian shakes his head. 'What I'm gonna do is make a note of my request and stick it in the case file. If there are bullet fragments in the rat's body, I want them.'

'Fuck off, Chigorin.'

'Nothing I'd rather do.' The Russian hands over the evidence bag containing the spent shell. 'I want this compared to the casings recovered on Hamilton Place,' he tells Boyle.

'I was there, remember.'

'I need the results right away, for obvious reasons.'

'Wait a minute.' Boyle produces a small

notebook and a pen. He opens the notebook and prints the word 'RUSH' in the center of a clean page. 'That's so I won't forget,' he tells Chigorin.

FOUR

The Russian arrives home at five o'clock. Home is an apartment he rents over a two-car garage in the Queens neighborhood of College Point. The apartment's only one room, but it's a big room, more like a loft, at least in the Russian's opinion. One thing for sure, he never feels claustrophobic when he's at home. And the furniture's half-assed decent, comfortable at least, if not exactly new. The one exception is a fifty-inch plasma flat-screen purchased only a month before. The set is connected to a satellite service that provides more channels than he can ever watch.

Though it's still early, the sky outside the window behind the television is already growing light. Chigorin lets the blinds down, then runs a finger along the slats to close them. He sets a glass containing four fingers of peppered vodka on the table next

44

to the couch, finally pushes the subway surveillance tape into his VCR. The VCR is twenty years old, but still functional, most likely because he never uses it, much preferring DVDs.

Chigorin drops on to a leather couch. The couch is even older than the VCR and its cracked cushions have long ago molded themselves to his ass. He picks up the remote, hits the PLAY button and settles back. The tape reveals the area to the right of the token booth, including the foot of the only set of stairs leading to the street, but not the platform where the shooting took place. That means he has to narrow the time frame. Otherwise, it's impossible to separate passengers who boarded a train from passengers on the platform when the shots were fired. He considers the situation for a moment before checking the telephone directory in his PDA for the number of the police liaison stationed at the Metropolitan Transit Authority.

Given the hour, Chigorin's expectations are not high, but when his call is answered on the third ring, he pounces.

'This is Detective Chigorin, Homicide Division. Who am I speaking to?'

'Sujan Chakraporty.' The man answers without hesitation, leading the Russian to conclude that he's given his real name.

'I need to know at what times, exactly, the 1 Train was in the station at a hundred and forty-fifth Street between three twenty and three forty.'

Chigorin endures the silence for a few seconds, then says, 'Look, Mr. Ch ... how do you say your name again?'

'Chakraporty.'

The Russian spells the name out. 'Is that the correct spelling?'

But Chakraporty's over his initial shock. 'Please, this is not my job,' he says, his tone flitting through several octaves.

'Well, you have to excuse me, but I dialed the number of the NYPD liaison and you, Mr. Chakraporty, picked up the phone.'

'I was expecting my wife to be the caller.'

'Your wife is a cop?'

'No, no.'

The Russian chuckles. 'Saving minutes on the old cell phone, right? Hey, I don't blame you. But you should get one of those plans with free minutes after nine o'clock. That way you won't have to use a city phone. Anyway, about my request.'

'This is not my job,' Chakraporty repeats. 'You must call back after nine o'clock please.'

'I can't do that, Sujan. This is a homicide investigation and I need the information now. And don't bullshit me, either. We both know you can get it for me in five minutes. Myself, I don't think that's too much to ask, but if you're of a different persuasion, you can put your supervisor on the phone.'

The Russian sips at his vodka while he studies the arrival/departure schedule Chakraporty was good enough to supply. The buildings on Hamilton Place closest to the crime scene still have to be canvassed, which can't happen until eight o'clock when the neighborhood wakes up. Also, the vic's relatives will have to be found, assuming he had any. Manuel Torres was carrying a single piece of identification at the hour of his death, a bogus Social Security card. But that's for later, too. For right now, he has the tape, a ready supply of vodka and no wish to sleep.

After a few minutes, the Russian constructs a simple timeline, which he records on a yellow pad. The murder on Hamilton

Place was called in at 3:25. A southbound 1 Train entered the station at 3:24 and left at 3:25. The subway shooting was called in by the token clerk at 3:37. A southbound 1 Train entered the station at 3:38 and left at 3:39.

The Russian isn't fond of assumptions. He much prefers his killers discovered still at the scene, murder weapon in hand. Either that or a dozen witnesses singing the identical song: 'Henry did it.' But in this case, the shooter was gone before the good guys rode up and no witnesses have as yet emerged. Not that he's giving up on the canvas. Maybe he'll get lucky, maybe some insomniac was looking out the window when Manuel Torres was assassinated.

But the Russian isn't holding his breath and he makes an assumption that significantly narrows his review of the tape. Chigorin assumes that every passenger standing on the southbound platform boarded the 1 Train that arrived at 3:24. Except for Homer. This doesn't have to be true and he knows it. Maybe somebody else was sleeping on the platform, somebody who woke up when the shooting started. Or maybe the shooter lingered on the platform for an extended period of time, waiting for a specific individual to arrive. Maybe those bullets were aimed at an enemy. Maybe the rat was an innocent bystander.

The Russian starts the time-stamped surveillance tape at 3:24, when the first train arrives, and runs it to 3:39 when the second train leaves the station. Then he runs it again, stopping the tape at various points to note each of the nine passengers entering the station. He gives the passengers names as he goes along, which makes them easier to remember: Skinny Kid, No Habla, Jail Bait One, Jail Bait Two, Chicken Hawk, the Headless Horseman, Satch, Old Gal and the Monk. Once he's able to keep them straight, he focuses on the passengers who exited the station after the shooting began. This is a more difficult task because the fleeing citizens are moving right along, even Old Gal, who walks with the aid of a cane. The Monk's been good enough to take her by the arm, but he's yanking her along like a dog at the end of a leash. The rest of the passengers are already up the stairs.

The Russian plays the tape several times, until he's certain. Nine passengers entered the station, but only seven left. The other two, Skinny Kid and the Headless Horseman, must have taken the southbound train that arrived at 3:38. Certainly, they were nowhere to be found when the first officers arrived at 3:42.

Skinny Kid is easy to identify because he stops within range of the camera for eighteen seconds before jumping the turnstile. He's no more than twenty and nondescript, a boy really, looking somehow small, though he probably stands a bit over six feet. The Russian, for no reason more pressing than the neighborhood's demographics, figures him to be Hispanic. West Harlem long ago ceased to be an all-black community. Dominicans and Mexicans now form a majority of its residents, a majority which continues to grow.

The Headless Horseman, on the other hand, presents the Russian with a serious problem. The grainy tape of Skinny Kid will yield a still photo the Russian can show around. But the Headless Horseman does not have a face. He's so big that his entire head is out of the frame. All Chigorin can say for sure is that the guy's Caucasian and has forearms that would shame Popeye. Plus, he's light on his feet, especially given his bulk. The man's chest is as big around as a refrigerator, but he moves with the confidence of a trained athlete.

The Russian's pretty much satisfied by the time his cell-phone rings at six thirty. He glances at the phone's little screen. It's his estranged wife, Yolanda, a Filipina nurse with a dependence problem. When she walked out on him two years before, taking little Sonia, the Russian didn't hold it against her. And he doesn't hold it against her now. He freely admits that he's cross-addicted to alcohol and work, and that he fully intends to remain that way until he's forced into retirement or his liver crashes. If he could, he'd probably walk out on himself. But he does resent Yolanda's calling on him every time a light bulb needs changing. It isn't as if she doesn't have a boyfriend.

'Yolanda, what's new?' Even as he answers, Chigorin's refilling his flask with peppered vodka.

'Are you working, Pete?'

'Yeah.' The Russian's hoping a terse reply will end the conversation. Fat chance.

'It's about Sonia. She's being bullied.'

Right away, Chigorin's put off. Yolanda has this way of being absolutely certain of

51

everything she says or thinks. There's no 'maybe' in her tone, no 'possibly'. Chigorin picks up his jacket, holds it to his face and sniffs. Not too rank.

'Isn't that the reason I paid to send her to karate school?' The Russian gets in a shot of his own. A registered nurse with a master's degree, Yolanda's income is half again as large as his, yet she calls on him whenever Sonia needs anything more than food on the table or clothes on her back.

'Well, that's the problem. It's taking place at the karate school.'

Chigorin jams the phone between his chin and his shoulder as he heads out the door. He knows that Sonia's a bit of a drama queen, but the thought of some pimple-faced asshole scaring her upsets him greatly. Not that he was ever the target of a bully. No, with the Russian, it was usually the other way around.

'A boy or a girl?'

'Pardon?'

'The bully. A boy or a girl?' Chigorin locks the door and heads for his car.

'A boy named Murray.' Yolanda rushes on before the interrogation continues. 'It's happening in this sparring they do, kumite. He's hitting her really hard. I've seen the bruises myself, on her chest and her sides. She's all black and blue, Pete.'

'What about Alexei?'

'Your cousin, the sensei?' Yolanda's tone oozes contempt. 'I spoke to him and he says taking punishment is part of the process. Myself, I think he likes it.'

The Russian has a notorious temper. Not only does he see red when he's angry, his neck and face turn the approximate color of an over-ripe tomato, a phenomenon which is happening right now as he walks toward his car. Chigorin's remembering the check he made out to his cousin, Alexei Barakova. He's remembering the check and Barakova's assurance: Don't worry, I protect my students.

'I'll take care of it,' he tells Yolanda.

'What're you gonna do, Pete?'

The Russian slides into the front seat of his Chevy Malibu and jams the key into the ignition. He reaches beneath the seat, removes a paper bag containing a fifth of vodka, lays it on the seat.

'I'm gonna get my money back and find Sonia another school,' he tells his wife. 'What did you think I was gonna do?'

'I thought you were gonna hurt Alexei. I mean, he's your cousin ...'

'All the more reason why he should have looked out for Sonia.'

The Russian's canvas of the buildings on Hamilton Place is thorough, if unproductive. He knocks on the door of every apartment with a view of the murder scene. Most of the individuals who respond are Latino, but Chigorin understands Spanish well enough to communicate. Only no one's talking. Or maybe nobody saw anything. He can't tell which. But in this case, it's the doing that counts, the doing and the paperwork generated by that doing.

On the way back to his car, the Russian stops long enough to call a detective named Soriani. Assigned to Missing Persons, Soriani passes his days at the morgue, matching bodies to names on a list. The Russian needs to contact Manuel Torres's relatives, but the name, even if genuine, is extremely common. Better to treat him as a John Doe and run his prints through the FBI's computer. In his early twenties, Torres had prison tattoos on his chest and both arms.

Soriani doesn't hesitate when the Russian

asks him to reclassify Manuel Torres. Until Soriani reformed, he and Chigorin were drinking buddies.

'You ever un-reform, I'm buyin' the drinks,' the Russian tells Soriani.

'You ever decide go on the wagon, I'll be your sponsor at AA.'

This is a bit the two of them have been doing for years.

The Russian slides the phone into his pocket. He's about to leave when he notices a shopping cart parked halfway down a set of stairs leading to the basement of the apartment building he's standing next to. The cart is stuffed with odds and ends: clothing, several books, a long-handled broom, a black trash bag half-filled with recyclable bottles and cans. But the Russian has no interest in the shopping cart, only in the tiny black man crouched behind it. He's looking down at the man and wondering if he maybe spent the night in the stairwell.

'Well,' he asks, 'you coming up or do I have to go down there and get you?'

'I could use some help with this cart,' the man admits. 'My arthritis is hurtin' me bad this morning.'

The Russian grabs the cart by the handle and yanks it up the stairs. 'You got a name?' he asks as he sets the cart down.

'Arthur.'

'Well, get on up here, Arthur. You got no excuses now.'

'No, sir.'

Arthur makes his way up the stairs, his progress slow. When he finally reaches the sidewalk, Chigorin realizes that the man's back is severely hunched, which is why he's so short. The Russian's just drunk enough to imagine having to live with a handicap this severe. It hurts him even to look at the man.

'I'm investigating a shooting. The one that took place last night.'

'That happened on the other block.'

'True enough, Arthur, but we know the shooter went directly to the subway station, which means he walked right past you.' This is a complete fabrication, but one unlikely to be challenged. 'I was wondering if you noticed him.'

'Well, I did and I didn't. I mean, I'm not exactly sure. I had a little bit to drink last night.'

'You and me both.' The Russian takes out

his flask and offers Arthur a quick hit, which Arthur gratefully accepts. 'Now, tell me what you remember.'

'I was down at the bottom of the stairs, tryin' to get to sleep, when I heard the shots. This bein' Harlem, gunfire ain't all that unusual and I didn't think too much of it. But then I heard footsteps, not runnin' exactly, but movin' pretty fast. Now I didn't get up or nothin' – I ain't crazy – and I never woulda got a look at that man if he hadn't walked close to the railing at the top of the stairs.'

Arthur pauses long enough to take a deep breath, then goes on. 'Man, I'm tellin' ya, this was the biggest white man I ever seen. This white man was a muthafuckin' giant.'

The Russian's pretty much exhausted. He's been on duty since midnight and it's now ten o'clock. But his work day is far from over. There's paperwork to be done and evidencc to be vouchered, tasks which keep him in Manhattan Homicide North's head-quarters until he signs out shortly after noon. The Russian wants to go directly from work to Anselm's Bar and Grill on College Point Boulevard. Anselm's is as close as he gets, or wants to get, to a social life. But there's a stop to make, at Sonia's karate school in Jackson Heights, and having to make it after a twelve-hour shift does not improve the Russian's mood. Not at all. He marches into the storefront school and walks across the dojo floor without taking off his shoes, marches right through a line of students and into Alexei's office, closing the door behind him.

Alexei is seated behind his desk, working on a spreadsheet. Though he's not a large man, not nearly as large as the Russian, he's skilled at his craft. The shelves behind his desk are lined with trophies. But there's something in Chigorin's eyes, not to mention the color of his face and the hair standing up on the top of his head, that compels Alexei to sound a temporizing note.

'Hey, cuz, is this about Murray and Sonia?' Alexei removes a bottle of Stolichnaya from a desk drawer. He pours a generous shot into a paper cup and offers it to Chigorin.

'I want my money back, right now.' The Russian's sorely tempted to slap the vodka out of his cousin's hand, Alexei's skills be damned. Karate school was supposed to be about Sonia overcoming her timidity and now she's more intimidated than ever.

'Yeah, well ... I don't have it right now. But I'll tell ya what, give me five minutes and I'll make the problem go away.'

'You should have made it go away when Yolanda spoke to you, not waited for me.' That said, Chigorin downs the cup of vodka. He pauses for a minute, until the fire rushes up into his brain, then gets to the point. 'If Sonia fails at karate, if she runs away and hides, she'll carry the loss with her for a long time. I trusted you to make sure that didn't happen.'

Alexei straightens in his chair. He's wearing a muscleman T-shirt beneath a black karate gi that reveals a nicely sculpted body. He's thinking that he could tear his cousin's head off, that Chigorin's so out of shape he's growing tits. But Alexei's always been intimidated by Chigorin, who's carrying a gun and who's crazy enough to use it if he feels threatened.

'Just watch for a minute, OK?'

Alexei stands up and leaves his office. He steps out on to the floor and circles around the class. The brown belt leading the class has separated the students into two rows. As one row steps forward to throw a reverse punch, their counterparts in the second row block the punch, then answer with a reverse punch to the chest. Even from the doorway, the Russian can see that no one's hitting anybody else very hard, a situation that changes abruptly when Alexei shakes his head and walks to the center of the practice floor.

'Murray, step out.'

Murray's heavy-lidded eyes fly open. He's maybe a couple of years older than Sonia, wearing a yellow belt, which makes him somewhat more proficient than the white belts in the class. But no match, of course, for Alexei. The Russian almost feels sorry for the kid.

'Reverse punch,' Alexei instructs, as he gets down into his stance. 'Give me all you've got.'

Yeah, right. Murray's punch comes in virtual slow motion, as if calculated not to give offense. Alexei brushes it aside and smacks the kid in the chest, a solid thump that reminds Chigorin of a blackjack slamming into a perp's kidney.

'Again,' Alexei orders.

The Russian doesn't wait around for the

end, though he's not entirely sure that Murray will get the message, which is several times removed from what's happening on the floor. Sonia's not even here. But the Russian's sure of one thing. Alexei will do everything in his power to ward off another visit from his cousin. And that's good enough for one day. Chigorin will definitely drink to that.

FIVE

Hootie doesn't want to get out of bed when he awakens at three o'clock in the afternoon. The mattress is incredibly comfortable and the sheets are as soft as a caress. Plus, there are all those worries out there, about his mom and his probation officer and his ongoing lack of gainful employment. The air conditioner is throwing out enough cold air to make a comforter mandatory, a comforter like the one snugged up under his chin. But Hootie knows he has to rise, not least because the odors wafting in from the kitchen are singing to him like the Sirens to Ulysses. Hootie knows about the Sirens because he read *The Odyssey* in tenth grade. That was before he got in with the wrong crowd, before he started smoking weed and snorting cocaine, before he started hanging out at the clubs.

Resigned, Hootie slips into the clothes he

wore on the previous day, the only clothes he has. He stops for a few minutes in the bathroom, brushing his teeth with his fingers. As he comes into the kitchen, Amelia greets him. She's sitting behind a stack of pancakes at the breakfast bar, looking very young. Behind her, a small TV is tuned to NY1, the cable news channel.

'Hi, how'd you sleep?'

'That mattress was unbelievable,' he finally admits.

Amelia and Bubba laugh. 'Hey, check this out,' Bubba says.

Hootie peers into a saucepan. He notes raspberries, blueberries and small chunks of mango bubbling away.

'You're making syrup.'

Bubba frowns. '*Compote*,' he corrects. 'I'm making a fruit compote to ladle over buttermilk pancakes enhanced with a touch of Grand Marnier. Plus, instead of buttering the pancakes, I'm using crème fraîche.'

Hootie doesn't know what crème fraîche is. He's thinking maybe that's the point. No matter what he told his mother about rejecting his black identity, he feels uncomfortable around white people. He just can't shake the sense that he's being judged, and harshly at that.

Bubba ladles pancake batter on to a cast-iron skillet. 'I started cooking when I was assigned to the kitchen at a minimum security joint up near the Hudson. The con who managed the kitchen was a restaurateur-conman named Allen Michaels. Talk about a jerk. Michaels didn't know his ass from his elbow about doing time and I had to jump in more than once to protect him. But he could really cook. He inspired me to start watching the Food Network. You know, Mario Batali and Rachael Ray.'

'Shit,' Amelia says, 'here comes the lecture. Hootie, pour yourself a cup of coffee and sit by me.'

Hootie fills a cup with coffee, adds sugar and cream. 'Gourmet coffee, right?'

'Tanzanian beans,' Bubba replies. 'Freshly ground.'

Hootie takes his coffee to the stool next to Amelia's. As he sits, she proffers a forkful of pancake and compote. Hootie accepts the offering – what else can he do? The tastes explode in his mouth. These are not his mother's pancakes. They did not come out of a box, nor have they been drenched with imitation maple syrup and smothered with butter.

'Whatta ya think?' Bubba edges a spatula beneath one of the pancakes on the griddle. He peers at the underside for a moment, then quickly flips it over.

'They're great.' Hootie's mouth is so filled with saliva that he nearly spits.

'So that's good, right? That I can really cook, that it's not bullshit?'

'Good for what?'

'For my image. See, when middle-class people look at me, people I'm hopin' to do business with, they see a big goon. I don't blame 'em, Hootie. Hell, I am a big goon. But I'm a goon who cooks. I'm a safe goon. I'm the goon who makes a mean risotto, a sumptuous coq au vin, a delectable crème caramel. So, yeah, maybe I committed this violent crime way back when, but I'm harmless now. Ordinary folks can deal with me.'

Bubba makes a shooting gesture with the fingers of his right hand. 'If you don't learn to make people feel safe, they won't do business with you.'

Hootie accepts another bite from Amelia. It does not disappoint. 'So I should maybe take up astrology?'

'The astrology bit is a little old. Nowadays, you can get a chart on the Internet for a few bucks. No, I got something better for you. What kind of Indian did you say you were?'

'Crow.'

'So learn everything you can about the Crow. Collect Crow memorabilia. Buy some jewelry. Memorize the stories. Become knowledgeable. Be interesting.'

Hootie gets the point. In order to become safe for white people, he'll have to become a professional Indian. He looks away for a moment, toward the glowing TV, just as the anchor introduces a story about a massacred rodent who closed down the 1 Line for three hours on the previous night. The reporter on the scene, an Asian woman with a pointy little chin named Indira Chitterjee, plays the story for laughs. She sobers only at the very end, when she declares that the police are trying to connect the hit on the rat to the murder of a suspected drug dealer on Hamilton Place.

'Awright, here we go.' Bubba flips Hootie's pancakes on to a plate, adds a thin layer of crème fraîche to each, finally ladles the compote on to the stack. Watching the performance, Hootie remembers the money

Bubba passed to Amelia. Seed money is what he'd called it.

'Chef Bubba, at your service.' Bubba lays the plate in front of Hootie, then retreats to the stove. He picks up a long wooden spoon, gives it a theatrical twirl and begins to prepare his own breakfast. 'There are three secrets to cooking: fresh ingredients, organization and experience. Now me, I was only joking before. I mean about being a chef. I'm like Rachael Ray. I cook, but I'm not a chef.'

Bubba finally slows down long enough for Amelia to get a word in. She pats Hootie on the shoulder and says, 'Don't worry, he shuts up when he eats.'

Hootie cuts into his pancakes with the edge of a fork. He's thinking Bubba wants him to know about the dealer on Hamilton Place. Bubba and Amelia, both. They want him to know that they're not fucking around.

Amelia cleans up after breakfast. She loads the dishwasher, cleans the stove and the table, takes a hand vac to the floor around Bubba's stool. Hootie and Bubba head off to the living room, where Bubba gestures to a facing pair of leather couches. The couches are armless, their cushions mounted on polished chrome frames.

'Hang on a second.' Bubba walks over to a closet near the front door. He plucks a box off the top shelf, carries it back to Hootie and lays it on a glass coffee table between the two couches.

'You know what this is?'

Hootie examines the side of the box. 'A Cuisinart?'

'Wrong. It's a Cookinart.'

Hootie takes a closer look, then smiles. 'It's a knock-off.'

'No, no. If it was a knock-off, it would say "Cuisinart" on the side of the box. The guy who designed this food processor wanted to compete with Cuisinart, especially on price. But it didn't work out.'

'What happened?'

Bubba smiles his happy-toddler smile, a parting of narrow lips revealing rows of neat square teeth. He puts the box to his ear and shakes it. 'They don't work, Hootie. They don't slice or chop or shred or mince or knead. Most of them don't, anyway. Oh, they'll turn on. They'll turn on and rotate like crazy, but the shaft that turns the cutting discs wobbles. So whatever you put into the unit ends up the consistency of a mash-ed potato. No surprise, right, that the ass-hole went bankrupt?'

Amelia strolls into the living room. She's carrying a fat joint in one hand, which she passes to Hootie. Then she opens the win-dow.

'The dude who owns this apartment,' she explains, 'you don't wanna get on his bad side.'

Hootie sucks on the joint. There's a trap here and he's falling into it. Already, he can't imagine going back out on the street. He offers the joint to Bubba, who declines.

'I got a game tonight,' he explains.

'Yeah, OK.' Hootie gestures to the still un-opened box. 'So, what does this bankruptcy have to do with Bubba Yablonsky?'

Bubba spreads his hands. 'Hootie, my boy, even as we speak, there's seven thousand Cookinarts sitting in a warehouse in New Hampshire. I can get my hands on them for a dollar apiece.'

'And then what?'

Amelia rolls her eyes. 'You'll be sorry.'

Bubba looks at her for a moment, his expression fond, and Hootie gets the impression they've done this bit before. 'Close your eyes a second, Hootie. Imagine a sweaty, middle-aged woman, maybe fifteen pounds overweight, preparing a meal in the kitchen. She's tired, she's cranky, her hair is mussed, her lipstick is smeared. Except for a small cutting board, the counter space is covered with vegetables, everything from string beans to zucchini, along with a variety of hard cheeses.'

Bubba's got the irritating telemarketer voice down pat, including the Aussie accent. 'Are you sick and tired of chopping and grating and slicing and dicing? Do you need a professional quality food processor, but can't afford to go out and spend two hundred dollars? Well, the Cookinart fourteen-cup food processor is the food processor for you. It does everything that hi-price processor does, not for two hundred dollars, or even one hundred dollars, but for a single payment of thirty-nine, ninety-nine. Yes, you heard me right. You get the Cookinart processor and four different blades for the unbelievably low price of thirty-nine, ninety-nine.'

Hootie takes another turn at the joint. He sucks the smoke deep into his lungs and holds it there. Two hits and he's already stoned, the weed so fresh the joint sticks to his fingertips when he hands it to Amelia.

'But wait,' Bubba cries. 'If you act today, we'll send you, absolutely free, a three-piece specialty disc set. A ninety dollar value absolutely free. That's a two hundred and ninety dollar value for only a single payment of thirty-nine, ninety-nine. But wait. For the first two hundred callers, we'll throw in a stainless steel holder for your discs, a sixty dollar value, absolutely free. That's a three hundred and fifty dollar value for only thirty-nine, ninety-nine. Call now while supplies last. Sorry, no CODs.'

Bubba settles back on the couch and Hootie applauds. 'That was crazy, Bubba. You could go on the air tomorrow.'

'Uh-uh.' Bubba shakes his head. 'Not me, Hootie. The agency that makes the spot will supply the actor. Remember, the machines don't work.' He leans forward, letting his elbows fall to his knees. 'Seven thousand units. We'll get forty bucks apiece for 'em, plus fifteen for shipping and handling. That's fifty-five dollars times seven thousand. That's three hundred and eighty-five thousand dollars. You hear what I'm sayin?

For thirty grand, total, I can purchase the units, make the spot and buy the air time. And you wanna hear the most beautiful part? The whole operation won't take more than three months. In and out, here and gone, so long and thanks for the money.'

Initially, Hootie finds himself with nothing to say. The burglaries that got him sent to Rikers Island netted him a grand total of three hundred dollars. Money spent so fast it was gone almost before he got it.

'Lemme tell ya,' Bubba continues, 'about a cellie I had in a minimum security joint upstate, a guy named Peter Talley, doing three years for fraud. Pete was an investment counselor. He convinced elderly widows to invest their life savings, young couples to establish college funds for their children, families to put up their homes. But he didn't invest in anything. He took their money – a grand total of five hundred thousand dollars – and he spent it. You listening close? Five hundred grand – three years. I knew dudes in Attica got seven years for burglary, fifteen-to-life for selling an ounce of coke to an undercover. And you wanna hear the funny part? Ten minutes after they hit the streets, they were back to committing the very same crimes in the very same ways. This, Hootie, is not gonna be my fate. I don't see any way to get ahead without taking a risk, but it's gonna be the least possible risk for the greatest possible gain.'

Amelia carries the joint to an ashtray on the window sill and stubs it out. She turns off the TV, turns on the stereo. Luther Vandross's seductive voice invades Hootie's body from every corner in the room, a specter in search of a soul. This is the stereo system he's wanted since he was old enough to want a system.

Hootie's expecting the big pitch. If there was ever a right moment, this is it. He's ready to say yes to anything short of murder. But it doesn't happen. Bubba rises. He looms over Hootie, his look almost regretful.

'I got a game in a few hours,' he explains. 'I gotta go.'

SIX

By the time Bubba retrieves his gym bag, it's all settled. Hootie and Amelia will hang out for a couple of hours, then come over to watch the game. Afterwards, all three will attend a private party at a club in Chelsea. The party is being thrown by a menfashion magazine celebrating its fifth anniversary.

Hootie feels hugely relieved when the door closes behind Bubba. He's not ready to make any decisions. But the last part of Bubba's monologue weighs on him. Hootie knows a number of third-strike offenders sentenced to long stretches for relatively petty crimes. And just like Bubba said, they went back to committing the same crimes as soon as the state let them out of prison. As if prison was the whole point.

Hootie recalls one of Eli Scannon's many lectures. 'The black man is a prisoner of his limited imagination. When he closes his eyes, he sees an original gangster playin' the fool in some music video, girls suckin' his dick and men kissin' his ass. The white man, he's hard-focused on the pot of gold at the end of the rainbow. He's not wearin' hip-hop and he doesn't have a gold rope around his neck. And the folks that kiss his ass? They're called maître d's, investment counselors, doormen, hotel managers, real estate salesmen. You listenin' to me? The black man uses fear to get respect. The white man buys respect.'

Even then, Hootie knew this wasn't altogether true. Scannon had a way of talking about the black man as if every black body was connected to a single brain. But there were black men out there, like his chump of a stepfather, who lived by the white man's rules, and lived well. What Scannon was really talking about was dumb-ass convicts like himself.

'Hootie, what're you thinkin'?'

Hootie opens his eyes to find Amelia offering the joint. He takes it and lights up. 'Thinkin' about my probation officer, how I'm gonna explain not havin' a job or a place to live. Say, you think I could borrow your phone?'

Amelia disappears into her room. She reappears a moment later and tosses a cell phone to Hootie, a burgundy Motorola Razr phone.

'It's got about fifteen minutes on it,' Amelia says. 'After you finish, come into my room. There's something I want to show you on the computer.'

Hootie waits until Amelia disappears, then dials his sister's cell phone. Two years out of law school, Teesha Hootier is the embodiment of everything he's not, the family success, a living reproach. Hootie loves his sister anyway. All through her teenage years, while their mother worked the night shift at Beth Israel Medical Center, Teesha had been the one to put groceries in the cupboard and meals on the table, to make sure he got his hair cut and that his Catholic school uniforms were clean and pressed for school.

'Yo, Teesha,' Hootie says when his sister answers. 'It's Hootie.'

'Hootie, Momma's worried sick about you.'

'Say what?' Hootie feels suddenly hot, as though at the onset of a fever. Damn that woman.

'Momma loves you.'

'Teesha, she threw me out the house. Hear what I'm sayin? She kicked me to the curb and now she's runnin' you some bullshit line about how she's worried sick. Man, that's cold.'

Teesha sighs into the phone. 'Even when we were children, I had to play the role of peacemaker. Tell me, have you found a job yet?'

'No, I—'

'Have you looked?'

'I'm only out a week.'

'Eight days,' Teesha corrects. 'So, tell me what you're doing. Were you on the street last night?'

Hootie lies without thinking twice. 'I rode the subway, but I'm at a friend's house now.' He lowers his voice to a whisper, though the room is empty. 'Only the thing about it is I can't stay here and I don't wanna go back on the street. I'm afraid I'll get picked up. I was wonderin' if I could stay by you?'

Teesha responds without hesitation, her tone cheerful. 'Not happening, brother. I'm assisting at a trial two days from now and I'll be working straight through. You need to go back to Momma's and make your peace.

What got into you anyway? You know that woman has buttons you just can't push.'

'She told you about the argument?' Hootie's growing angrier by the minute. Grind you down was what Bubba said. Just go on home, tell your mother and her asshole husband that you were wrong. Tell 'em you're a black man, for now and forever. Tell 'em you'll be whatever they want you to be. And don't forget to grin.

'Hootie, I don't care if you grow your hair long enough to cover your ass. But there are things you have to do first, like get a job and find a place to live. Like become independent. You know how Archie gets about his house and his rules. Anyway, baby, you can't stay here. The couch is covered with briefs.'

Briefs? Hootie's talking about his whole life. Because there's a big fat choice looming on the horizon, and if it's between Bubba's scam and returning to his mother's apartment, he's pretty sure which way he's gonna go.

'Awright, Teesha, I'll be speakin' to ya.'

'Look, Hootie, I'm also worried about you. I'm thinking that if you can't live with the rules at Momma's, what will you do the first time a boss gets up in your face? And bosses will do that, Hootie. They'll chew you out and expect you to submit. That's just the way it is.'

'You're telling me I should know my place?'

'If you don't, somebody will damn well show it to you. It could be a boss. It could be Archie. It could be a cop or a corrections officer. You choose, baby brother.'

Hootie's pretty much blown away by the time he finally hangs up and heads off to join Amelia. He doesn't know what he's expecting when he comes through the door, but what he finds does not restore his sobriety. Fluff and flounce everywhere. Ruffled curtains, ruffled bedspread, tasseled pillow cases, shaggy rug, all in shades of blue, from cobalt to baby blue to an armchair upholstered in midnight-blue velvet. This is the perfect room for Amelia. It plays to a self-mockery Hootie's only beginning to sense. But it's not her room, of course. The whole apartment is borrowed.

Amelia's sitting before a laptop computer. She gets up when he enters and gestures for him to take her chair. Amelia's wearing cut-off jeans and a Baby Phat top with the company logo, a sitting cat, done in glitter. Designed for an adult, the top droops across her flat chest. But Amelia will never find clothes to fit her, not unless she shops in the little girls' department.

'My big performance, Hootie. Welcome to the show.'

Amelia's big performance is a ten-minute streaming video from a page on myTime, a page supposedly created by a precocious twelve-year-old named Veronica. Amelia's head and shoulders fill the monitor, a cute girl, though not beautiful, with a pixie haircut, big blue eyes and enough makeup to shame a Hunts Point whore. Instinctively, Hootie recoils, but then he feels Amelia's hand on his back.

'Don't freak out,' she instructs. 'Just take it in.'

The makeup is reasonably well applied, but the colors might have been chosen by a narcissistic chimpanzee. Pink lips, green eye shadow, bright red circles of rouge. Amelia's false eyelashes are preposterously long and her arched brows extend halfway to her hairline.

The little girl in the video adjusts the camera, then sits back in her chair. She's wearing a cheerleader's outfit, pink blouse and short blue skirt. When she crosses her legs, the skirt rides up to mid-thigh.

Suddenly, she looks to her right and says, 'Stop it, Melissa.' This followed by a giggle, followed by a determined sobering.

'Hi, my name is Veronica and I live in New York City.'

Veronica goes on to recite a laundry list of favorite singers and favorite movies. The singers include Little Kim, Beyonce, Mary J. Blige, Janet Jackson and the elder stateswoman of sexual innuendo, Madonna.

'My ambition,' she announces, with a straight face, 'is to be a dancer in music videos.'

Veronica's favorite movies are mostly chick flicks. Chick flicks are all about sex, but just in case the casual viewer misses the point, Veronica explains that her favorite thing of all time is *Sex in the City*, a television series. When the show went off the air, she nearly died, of course, but she's seen the movie four times.

Throughout this recitation, Veronica keeps glancing to her right, at a friend hidden off-camera. Lots of giggles. Lots of 'noooooo!' and 'awesome' and 'will you please stop' and 'shuuuut uuuuuup!'.

Finally, a serious look, aimed directly at the camera. 'Melissa wants me to do my cheerleader routine.' A theatrical sigh, accompanied by a rolling of the eyes. 'Alright, OK. But don't blame me if I fall on my face.'

It's all there. The leg kicks, the splits, finally the cartwheels. Glimpses galore of slightly oversized cotton panties. White, naturally.

Hootie can't take his eyes off the monitor. He's repulsed and admiring at the same time. Veronica is entirely believable. Sexually curious, but ignorant as well, her makeup so inappropriate it could only have been applied by an innocent hand.

'It's fucking brilliant,' Hootie says. 'And I know what's coming next.'

Amelia smiles agreeably. 'I've been exchanging emails with the mark for about a month now and I've spoken to him on the phone a couple of times. He's a civil engineer, lives in Whitestone. Hootie, the man is so hot he's melting. Here, check this out.'

Sure-handed, Amelia brings up a folder containing several dozen emails, both sent and received. She clicks on one and the text jumps on to the screen.

Hootie reads the first line: *You say that you let your girlfriend's brother get to third base...*

That's enough for Hootie. 'You're tellin' me that you're just gonna fuck this chicken hawk?'

'Are you upset?'

'Damn right.'

Amelia shakes her head. 'Hootie, what happened to me in my life, this is nothing.' The look in Amelia's eyes is now positively maternal. 'Think about it, Hootie. If thirty thousand can become three hundred and fifty thousand, what can three hundred and fifty thousand become?'

'That's Bubba's song and dance. That's *his* fucking bait.'

'Not true. I costed the operation myself. For thirty grand, we can drop into the deep South, where consumer protection laws are non-existent, and market our product to several million consumers. Hootie, we've only got seven thousand units to peddle. The math speaks for itself.'

'And what happens when our ... our consumers go to the cops? Maybe Alabama doesn't have consumer protection laws, but this is outright fraud.'

Amelia grins. 'First thing, we tell customers, in tiny print of course, that delivery takes four to six weeks. Then we demand they try out the units in their own homes for thirty days before shipping them back for a complete refund. Only problem is that the refund takes up to ten weeks to process. So do the math again. Six weeks plus four weeks plus ten weeks. That's five months, by which time we'll be long gone. And the best part is that nobody gets hurt. Yeah, the marks are out fifty-five dollars. But we're not forcing some granny to sell her house and move into a nursing home.'

Hootie finally catches his breath. He sees where this is going and when he speaks, his voice is almost wistful. 'And the cops won't investigate because the amount is too small.'

'There you are, Hootie. As white-collar crimes go, the money we're talkin' about is nothin' but chump change.'

They make a stop on the way to the game, at an outdoor ATM on Avenue A. The machine is fastened to the outer wall of a bodega with a pair of thick steel straps bolted to the wall. But while the company that placed the ATM has taken care to protect the machine, it's ignored the interests of the general public. There's no surveillance camera.

The credit card Amelia gives to Hootie has raised numbers on one side and a magnetic strip on the other. Otherwise it's a blank sheet of white plastic.

'Here's the PIN number.' Amelia hands over a Post-it note with a six-digit number written across its face. 'Take out three hundred. A hundred for me and Bubba – we had to buy the card – and two hundred for you.'

Hootie accepts the card and the note. 'And the best part,' he observes, not without a certain amount of sarcasm, 'is that nobody gets hurt.'

'That's right. When the transaction is reported, the banks will credit the account and eat the loss.'

Hootie inserts the card, enters the PIN number and collects his cash. Now, as he and Amelia stroll uptown, he's got money in his pocket. And although he tells himself to slow down, he feels stronger for having even this small roll. There's a voice in his head now, persistent and insinuating. The voice tells him that what Bubba and Amelia plan to do is called blackmail, and that the penalty for blackmail is harsh. Nor, the voice insists, will any judge be likely to show mercy on sentencing day – not when they plan to leave a pedophile free to victimize other children.

And what about that? Can Hootie live with himself afterward? True, the voice explains, you're not the most law-abiding person in the world. But there are still lines you don't cross and the line marked 'chicken hawk' is one of them.

They're approaching 14th Street, walking past a little mountain of garbage set by the curb. The evening is sultry and oppressive, and Hootie instinctively chokes off a breath as his nostrils are assaulted by the smell of rotting meat. The Lower East Side is home to an army of young professionals come to make it big in the Big Apple. They arrive unattached for the most part, still young enough to work all day and party into the night, to ignore garbage and weather both. The sidewalks are crowded, the chatter bright with promise, the outdoor cafes standing room only.

Hootie tries to imagine himself among them. Though mostly white, there are a scattering of blacks, Latinos and Asians, so race isn't really a factor. But these people belong to a different world. His sister, yeah. He can imagine Teesha and her lawyer friends gossiping away over drinks and dinner. But not him.

'When do I find out what you want from me?' he finally asks.

'I guess right now's good enough.' Amelia pauses to take a deep breath. 'Bubba and me, we're freaks. We can't front the operation. But you, Hootie, put you in a pair of Dockers and a polo shirt, maybe a Yankees cap and a pair of worn Nikes, and you could be anyone.'

Now it makes sense. Hootie out front, his signature on every document, his face before every potential witness, his name on the indictment.

'Lemme see if I have this right. You and Bubba stay in the background, ready to disappear in a minute, while I take the risks.'

Amelia's laughter is genuine. 'Disappear? Bubba? Hootie, when you're six-ten and weigh two hundred and seventy-five pounds and you've been to prison for manslaughter, there's no disappearing. As for me, there are only about a hundred people in the country who have Kallmann syndrome. Plus, I can't buy a drink in a restaurant, no matter how much ID I show, can't rent a car, even with a credit card, or lease an apartment or buy plane tickets unless I buy them online. So there's no disappearing for me either.'

On 15th Street, they approach four security guards standing before the side entrance to a school. A trickle of fans enters the school, passing between the guards and through a set of metal detectors. One man sets off an alarm and is quickly frisked.

'Why me?' Hootie asks. 'There have to be a thousand people out there who ... who could be anyone.'

'This morning, before you got up, I asked Bubba the same question. I told him, "You don't even know this kid. He could be completely unreliable."'

'So, what did he say?'

'That you're young enough to adapt to a new way of thinking. The others, the guys he did time with, are locked into whatever they did to get them convicted in the first place.' Amelia hesitates for a moment, gathering her thoughts. Finally, she says, 'Bubba came up hard. His mother was a fall-down drunk and a whore to boot, so he basically raised himself. Now he's lookin' for a family, but he's not stupid enough to think he can have one in the traditional way. Right this minute, I'm his family. If you decide to come in with us, you'll be his family, too. And something else you should consider. Bubba was in his junior year at St. John's when he killed that kid, maintaining a three-point-eight average. There was even talk of a Rhodes Scholarship to Oxford. I know he's smarter than I am, and he's probably smarter than you are, too.'

'That,' Hootie declares as they are passing through the metal detectors, 'is exactly what I'm afraid of.'

SEVEN

The gym is packed ten minutes before the opening tip, but no one's sitting down. The atmosphere is highly charged, the crowd strictly ghetto. There's enough hip-hop gear to fill a FUBU warehouse, enough gold to excite a conquistador. Everyone's betting everyone else, as at a dog or cock fight, and the players have the look of seasoned warriors. And they are warriors, Hootie realizes, school-yard warriors, their skills honed by years of play on concrete courts all over the city.

'See that dude in the wheelchair?' Amelia asks.

'Yeah.'

'That's Montague. He sponsors the team. Montague got himself shot a couple of years ago, which is why he's in the chair. The two men standing next to him are his bodyguards.'

Montague is a small black man whose

muscle-bound guardians would dwarf him even if he could stand. Still, they appear small compared to Bubba, who leans down to speak with their boss.

Amelia leads Hootie through the crowd, stopping to speak with this man or that woman. Everyone seems to know her, and to treat her with respect, the men especially. And why not? Amelia is simply not forgettable, just as she said. Plus, Bubba's her guardian.

The teams wear uniforms purchased at the NBA store, the red and orange of the Knicks and the Kelly-green of the Boston Celtics. Bubba's a Knick and his uniform bears the name and number of Charles Oakley, power forward in the Patrick Ewing era. This comes as a puzzle to Hootie, since Bubba's playing center. But when the game begins, Bubba's reasoning becomes obvious. Charles Oakley wasn't the most talented of the Knicks' players, but he made up for it with stamina and hustle. He dove for every loose ball, fought for every rebound and was likely to crack your skull if you encountered him in the paint. Fouls be damned, that area of the court belonged to him.

Bubba makes the terms clear on the Celtics' second possession when their point guard drives to the basket. The collision is hard enough to silence the crowd, the referee's whistle incredibly sharp in the hushed atmosphere. If Bubba hadn't gotten a piece of the ball, he'd most likely be called for a flagrant foul. As it is, the Celtics' guard is awarded a pair of shots. He makes both and never challenges Bubba again.

Nor do any of the other Celtics, including their center, who's unable to control Bubba at either end of the court. The first time Bubba handles the ball, he simply backs the man down before slamming the ball through the hoop. This happens again before the Celtics decide to swarm Bubba, a tactic which should free one of his team-mates to cut to the basket. None does, settling instead for outside jumpers when Bubba passes out to the free man.

And so it goes, throughout the first half and the third quarter. The Celtics shoot from outside because they're afraid to challenge Bubba. The Knicks shoot from outside because ... Hootie finally gets to the because part during the half-time break. Bets are being negotiated all around him.

This isn't like the pros or the college ranks, with an official point spread and no betting after the game begins. Here, it's every man for himself.

'What was the point spread before the game?' Hootie has to speak directly into Amelia's ear to make himself heard.

'Nine.'

Amelia's quick grin demonstrates a certain amount of pride. The Celtics are up four points and the spread has diminished from nine points to three. Bubba and his boys have been shaving points all along, keeping the game close to bring the point spread down.

The Celtics are still up six as the Knicks' guard brings the ball down the court at the opening of the fourth quarter. He wastes no time passing to Bubba, and even less time cutting to the basket. Bubba hits him just as he crosses the foul line. From there, it's only a step to an easy lay-up.

Hootie has to give the Celtics credit. After the Knicks score six straight points to tie the game, they make an adjustment. Their center drops into the paint as soon as one of the Knicks cuts to the basket. This leaves the Celtics' shooting guard, who's maybe six-one, to guard Bubba. Talk about no fuckin' contest. Bubba sinks a fifteen-foot jumper, then another on the next possession, then a third.

The crowd goes crazy, the noise jackhammer loud. Somehow, they all appear to be rooting for Bubba, some even chanting his name: *Bub-BA, Bub-BA.* And Bubba, he's got the game face on and he's taking whatever they give him, passing, shooting or going to the basket. The Celtics manage to stay in the game only because their shooters get hot, especially their two-guard, who knocks down a series of jumpers coming off the pick. But these are not NBA superstars. They cool off six minutes into the quarter and the Knicks pull away to win by eight.

As his teammates head for the locker room and the crowd files out, Bubba sits alone on the bench, a towel draped over his head. Accompanied by his bodyguards, Montague guides his motorized wheelchair across the court to join him. Montague's too far away for Hootie to hear the words he speaks, but they must be encouraging because Montague pats Bubba's shoulder before passing over a small roll of bills. The bills disappear into Bubba's massive right hand as Montague drifts away. Now Bubba is entirely alone, bent forward, his elbows on his knees, hands to his face. The towel masks his expression and he looks, to Hootie, like a defeated man.

Hootie makes his way to the bench and sits down alongside Bubba. He wants to offer some observation, but he can't find the words and it's Bubba who speaks first.

'You wanna hear a story?' he asks.

'Sure.'

'You know how, in the institution, one of the first things you look to do is enroll in a program?'

'Hell, yes. When you come up for parole, the board looks for proof that you've been rehabilitating yourself. I enrolled in a carpentry class first chance I got.'

Bubba begins to unwind the elastic bandages that encase his knees. 'There aren't all that many programs in Clinton. Clinton's more about punishment. So when they shipped me there a few weeks after I was sentenced, the only open program was called Anger Management. Lemme tell ya, Hootie, I was resistant. For the first few weeks, I barely listened. But then it finally hit me. I'm talkin' about everything I threw away. And for what? To avenge my honor? When I thought about what the jerk actually said, the exact words and my insane response ... it was like I kept getting smaller and smaller, the incredible shrinking basketball star.'

Hootie nods agreement. Bubba's competitors, on both the Knicks and the Celtics, were excellent school-yard basketball players. They handled the ball well and they could shoot. But they were several notches below Bubba. And if that's true, given that Bubba's closing in on thirty years old, how good was he ten years ago?

'Never again,' Bubba says. 'I practiced every exercise the group leader gave me. I learned to read the signs before I lost my cool, to stop the process. Believe me when I tell you that the Clinton Correctional Facility is a place where you can easily go ballistic. You get provoked all the time. Staying cool became like a passion, like when I was a kid shooting baskets after dark. At the end of every workout, I took a shot from mid-court. If I missed, I tried again, and again, and again, until I finally made one. No matter how long it took, no matter how tired I was.'

Hootie nods to himself, imagining Bubba throwing up shot after shot, fetching the ball, setting up again. 'So, did it work? I'm talkin' about the anger thing?'

'Yeah, it did. I still get mad sometimes, but only in private. If you see me pissed-off in a public situation, you can bet that I'm acting. Now, whatta ya say we go out and party?'

Hootie watches Bubba cross the court on his way to the locker room. Hootie's thinking about a dead drug dealer on Hamilton Place and a dead rat on a subway platform. Thinking there was no anger, thinking the dealer was step number three in a ten-steps-to-success program. As for the rat, Hootie doesn't have a clue.

The party is held in an enormous loft in what used to be the garment district. There's nothing fancy about the club. A floor has been removed to create a high ceiling and there's a glass-topped bar along the wall furthest from the main entrance. The rest of the space is reserved for a dance floor constantly swept by spotlights mounted on the ceiling. The floor is packed when the security guards at the front unhook the velvet rope to admit Hootie, Bubba and Amelia.

The music is strictly techno, which Hootie's never liked, and predictably loud, and nobody seems to be dancing with anybody else. Hootie's content to remain on the sidelines. He plucks a grilled shrimp from a platter of hors d'oeuvres carried by a female waiter sporting a tuxedo jacket over a white T-shirt. Wrapped in bacon, the shrimp is delicious and he washes it down with a glass of red wine snared from a second, identically dressed waiter. Still, he can't relax. The party is being thrown by an upscale fashion magazine and there are costumes galore, from tattered lace to emerald boas. Everybody hip, everybody cool, everybody safe. Uptown, any visit to a club entails a certain amount of risk. You brush the wrong dude's shoulder and a second later you're throwin' punches. And that's only if he doesn't have a weapon. But not here. Here, when you step on some punk's shoes, you say, 'Excuse me.'

Hootie's thoughts remain critical. He tells himself it's all too cold, as mechanical as the techno music pouring from enormous speakers on either side of the room. The dancers have no steps, no moves – they bounce up and down, stiff as wind-up toys. All he can think about is leaving.

But then Amelia sidles up to where he stands, tucked back in the shadows. She offers him a tab of ecstasy and he doesn't hesitate. He flips the tab into his mouth and chases it with a flute of champagne. Thirty minutes later, he's on the floor, bouncing up and down like the rest of the assholes. He has no choice; the energy coursing through his flesh is uncontainable. And the music's finally making sense, all the whoops and whistles, the beat so steady it could only have been created by a machine.

At some point, Hootie finds himself dancing with an Asian girl wearing a ruffled blouse and a pair of white shorts brief enough to reveal an inch of buttock on either side. They begin five feet apart, two strangers making random eye contact, then move together, the space between them slowly dissolving until they rub against each other's bodies and Hootie's as hard as he's ever been in his life. He doesn't know what he's gonna do about it, not unless she has an apartment somewhere, but then she takes his hand and leads him down a long corridor to a small room at the back of the club. The room smells of sex and the narrow bed is none too clean, neither of which bothers Hootie all that much. The girl's hands are on his belt before the door closes. A moment later, she's unzipping his fly and sliding his pants and underwear to the floor. He rises to the tips of his toes when her mouth closes around his cock, then finally tumbles back on to the bed. Thinking, Damn you, Bubba. Damn you, damn you, damn you.

Afterwards, just before the girl leaves, she tells him that he has a really nice body.

EIGHT

Detective Chigorin begins his day in the bathroom, where he relieves himself and brushes his teeth before reaching into the medicine cabinet for a bottle of Prevacid. The fire in his belly doesn't burn as hot at it once did. There's no devil poking his gut with a molten pitchfork, merely a smoldering reminder that a major life question still to be answered is whether his stomach will give out before his liver. The doc who treated the Russian's original complaint, a Haitian named David Pierre, wanted to shove a tube down his throat and into his stomach. Chigorin agreed initially, but then cancelled at the last minute. The Prevacid was working fine. As for the rest of it, he didn't want to know, and still doesn't.

After a quick shower, Chigorin dons a freshly dry-cleaned suit, a short-sleeved white shirt and a new green tie he discovers in the back of his closet. Before heading out to his car, he jams his laundry, including a pair of dirty suits, into a red laundry bag. It's only a few blocks to College Point Boulevard and the Lucky Fortune Laundromat where he deposits the red bag.

Chigorin performs these simple tasks in a fog. He's not exactly hung-over. There's no headache and he doesn't feel nauseated. He just needs a drink to attain the degree of alertness most people call normal, a drink he's chosen to obtain at Anselm's Bar and Grill, only two doors away from the laundry. That drink, a shot of citrus-flavored vodka poured from a bottle stored in Anselm's freezer, is sitting on the bar when the Russian comes through the door.

'I seen ya park the car, lad.' A few years older than the Russian, Anselm Deenihan, Jr. was shipped out to the University of Dublin after graduating from Holy Cross High School in Bayside. Anselm dwelt in the land of his ancestors for two years – happy years, or so he claims – before returning upon the sudden death of his father. After the wake and the funeral, Deenihan abruptly abandoned his studies, opting instead to run the family bar. He didn't have much choice, given the mother and three younger siblings to be fed and clothed. But if Anselm Deenihan never got an education in the old country, he did retain a memento of his time in Ireland, an Irish lilt that he's hung on to for thirty years.

'No explanation necessary.' Chigorin downs the shot and smiles. Already, things are looking up.

Anselm leans over the bar and half-whispers, 'Herself was here looking for ya.'

'When?'

'Yesterday.'

'Damn.'

Herself is Maureen McDonald, who waitresses at a diner on Astoria Boulevard. She and the Russian are something of an item, and the Russian's sorry he missed her because he's been horny all week. His first instinct is to call her and he takes out his phone. But then he checks himself. Maureen's the decider in their relationship, always has been. Plus, apart from the sex, he's pretty sure that she doesn't like him.

Now that he has the phone out, Chigorin decides to make a couple of business calls. He gestures to Anselm for a refill. 'You got anything to eat?'

'Salami. You want a sandwich?'

Anselm's is a workingman's bar tucked into the obscure neighborhood of College Point. Once home to better-off white workers, College Point is slowly gentrifying, a fact Deenihan predictably bemoans. Al's been plowing the same ground for so many years that he resents the very concept of change. If he could, he'd take the word out of the dictionary. Just as he'd take the word 'grill' off the sign outside if it wasn't attached to the word 'bar'. There's no grill in his bar and there never will be. Potato chips, pretzels, peanuts? Fine. Other than that, unless you're a very old customer like Chigorin, you have to bring your food with you and eat it off the bar.

Chigorin shudders, salami not being his first choice for what amounts to breakfast. But Dr. Pierre was insistent the last time Chigorin saw him. Don't drink on an empty stomach.

'Salami's good.'

Deenihan lays eight slices of Genoa salami on a slice of rye bread. He slathers the meat with hot mustard, adds a second slice of bread and passes the sandwich to Chigorin on a paper plate. The Russian supposes that he should be grateful. Most afternoons, he has to settle for bologna or liverwurst.

Chigorin takes a bite, chases it with his second drink of the day, then dials Nick Soriani's cellphone number. 'Nick, it's the Russian. Did I wake you?'

Soriani groans. 'Don't you check your messages? I called three hours ago.'

Though Chigorin hasn't checked his messages – too often they're from superior officers – he isn't apologetic. In fact, when Soriani hangs up, he finds himself miffed. He saved Nick's ass more than once back when they were partners.

'Some guys have no gratitude,' he informs Anselm, who's ferrying a pitcher of beer to a pair of construction workers seated at a table near the front of the bar. The Russian looks down at his sandwich. He's gearing himself up to take another bite when the door opens to admit Harry Gurstein bearing a pizza. Gurstein is a retired high school teacher with a thirst to match Chigorin's own.

The Russian pushes his sandwich to one side as he retrieves his three phone messages. The first two are from Yolanda. Sonia wants to go to a soccer camp in August;

please send money. The third was left by Soriani. The Hamilton Place victim has been positively identified. His name is Ramon 'Flaco' Almeda, not Manuel Torres, and he has a long rap sheet that includes possession of cocaine with intent to distribute. His last known address is on West 162 Street, a mile from where he died.

'Pizza?'

The Russian looks up at Harry Gurstein. Harry's got his usual on the bar in front of him – a shot of Jack Daniel's, neat, and a bottle of Budweiser. He's a tall, skinny man with the permanently reddened cheeks of a professional drinker.

'Yeah, gimme a minute.'

Hoping he's on a roll, Chigorin dials up the police lab in Long Island City. He gets through to Ballistics after a bit of a struggle with the phone menu, only to find that a comparison between the shells casings found at the murder scene and the one found in the subway station has yet to be made. Chigorin's first instinct is to threaten, but he knows that a display of temper will only work against his aim.

'C'mon,' he wheedles, 'gimme a break here. This is a homicide investigation. There is a murderer walkin' the streets.'

The woman on the other end of the line doesn't laugh, not exactly. But she's clearly amused. 'What're you sayin' here, Detective? That you're ready to make an arrest if the casings match?'

A good point, which the Russian has to admit. What he's got is a giant white man who's yet to be identified.

'You wouldn't consider tellin' me how long before you make the comparison?'

'I have good news and bad news, Detective. The good news is that we prioritize homicide and rape cases. The bad news is that there was a spike in homicides over the weekend, so we're backed up. Try me tomorrow afternoon.'

His errands run, at least for the present, Chigorin settles down to his breakfast, pizza topped with peppers and onions. He's on his second slice when herself walks into the bar. Two inches taller than the Russian, Maureen McDonald was a great beauty in her youth. But that was fifteen years and thirty-five pounds ago. Now her forehead and cheekbones have pushed forward to dominate her pug nose and thin mouth, and her blue eyes are angry and resentful. Nevertheless, as far as the Russian's concerned, Maureen's a pure winner simply because their occasional afternoons are utterly without pretense. Maureen refers to what they do as screwing or fucking. The phrase 'making love' has never passed her lips.

'You want a drink?' Chigorin asks.

'Thanks, but I don't have time. I'm covering for one of the girls and I gotta be at work in a couple of hours.'

Tight timeline be damned, Chigorin makes a stop at a liquor store on the way to Maureen's apartment. Maureen's sitting next to him, her skirt midway between her knees and her crotch. She's staring directly at him, projecting that I'm-gonna-fuck-your-brains-out look she gets when she's really horny. The Russian can't take his eyes off her legs and he bangs his head climbing out of the car.

'Do you want me to kiss that and make it better?' Maureen asks.

The Russian stands there for a minute, staring down at her knees. 'Actually,' he tells her. 'I'd heal faster if you raised your skirt another few inches.'

Blurred by haze and smog, the sun is still high enough to clear the apartment buildings on West 162nd Street when Chigorin parks his car at seven o'clock in the evening. He reaches beneath the seat for the vodka bottle and takes a quick swig. The Russian's come in search of Flaco Almeda's family, and his first priority is to inform them of Flaco's death. But he's not unmindful of the fact that one of them might have pulled the trigger. Giant white man or not.

The building Chigorin approaches, between Broadway and Amsterdam Avenue, is typical of West Harlem's apartment houses. Marble half-columns flank the door in front and there's a frieze between the third and fourth floors that runs across the brick. This is proof positive that the structure was originally built for reasonably upscale renters, back a hundred years ago when Harlem was a Jewish neighborhood. But there's evidence of neglect everywhere, from the scaffolding over the sidewalk, to the broken intercom, to the broken locks on a front gate and at the front door, to the broken elevator.

The lobby smells of cooking, of garlic and cilantro and steaming rice, as do the stairs

Chigorin climbs to the third floor. He's heading for apartment 3G and he doesn't have to guess where it is. An open door to his left reveals a crowded apartment and there are people, men, women and children, milling about in the hallway. A birthday party? The Russian doesn't think so. He thinks the grapevine beat him to the punch and he's arrived just in time for the wake, body or no body.

Everyone looks at him as Chigorin approaches the door. That he's a cop – and an annoyed cop at that – is more than obvious. How is he supposed to conduct interviews under these conditions? He takes out his badge and attaches it to the lapel of his jacket. It's hot as hell and his torso is slick with sweat. For sure, he won't be able to wear this suit again tomorrow.

Chigorin passes through the front door and into a crowded living room. He pauses just long enough to spy a woman sitting on a camelback couch. Flanked by two older women, she's perched in the center of the couch, one buttock on either cushion, accepting condolences. Chigorin addresses her in broken Spanish. He introduces himself and offers his own condolences before asking if she's related to Ramon Almeda. To his relief, she responds in English.

'I am his mother.'

'I'm sorry for your loss, *senora*.' He pauses long enough to evaluate his situation. There are more than a dozen people in the room and they're all watching him. What's more, it's obvious that a few are in the life. Just as it's obvious that he'll have to come back tomorrow. And that's what he tells her.

'I'm investigating your son's death and I need to speak to you in private,' he explains. 'Suppose I come back tomorrow morning?'

'My mother is too upset. You can speak to me.'

Chigorin spins on his heel to face a short Latino in his mid-twenties. Already balding, the man wears a thin beard that covers a myriad of small acne scars.

'And you are?'

'Hector Almeda. I'm Ramon's brother.'

'Well, I'm glad to meet ya.' The Russian extends his hand and Hector has no choice except to take it. Hector's wearing a Transit Authority uniform with a tag that reads, 'MOTORMAN'. He's the good son.

'Ya know, we can kill two birds with one stone,' Chigorin says. 'We can drive down to the Medical Examiner's for you to make a formal identification and we can talk along the way.' He bestows what he believes to be a concerned look on Hector's grieving mother. 'Right now, your mom has enough problems.'

The Russian glances at the other mourners in the room. They're impressed, he can tell, with his respectful attitude. They look to Hector's mom, who looks to Hector, who frowns first, then nods.

'I have to report for work by ten o'clock,' he tells Chigorin.

'No, problem, Hector. In fact, I'll drive you myself.'

NINE

Chigorin takes his time on the ride to the morgue on East 30th Street. Rather than FDR Drive, or even the West Side Highway, he drifts along Broadway to West 96th Street, then cuts east to 2nd Avenue before heading south again. The traffic isn't particularly heavy, except near the 59th Street Bridge, but there are lights on every corner and their progress is necessarily slow. Chigorin has the windows rolled up tight and the air conditioning on high, locking himself and his passenger into the narrow confines of the car's interior. Other cars move around them, but except for the occasional horn, the only sound they hear, besides each other's voices, is the whoosh of the air conditioner's fan.

Prompted by Chigorin, Hector begins by asserting that the Almeda family has always been close. As the Russian's never met a

Latino from any country who doesn't make the identical claim, this does not come as news. Nor does any of what follows, not until the very end.

The patriarch of the family, Hector explains, Luis Almeda, came to the United States from the Dominican Republic illegally in 1971 at the age of fourteen. Over the next thirty years, he married and produced three children. Ramon was the youngest, Hector in the middle, Celia, now on her third tour of duty in Iraq, the oldest.

'My father worked his ass off, Detective. He always had two jobs, and sometimes three. He cleaned hospital floors, delivered newspapers at six o'clock in the morning, worked construction, mowed lawns in the suburbs. My mother wasn't far behind him. She cleaned apartments all day, then came home to care for her own children. And neither one of them ever made more than ten bucks an hour, no time-and-a-half for overtime, no holidays, no vacation, no sick days.'

The Russian nods along as Hector makes his points, although he's not particularly sympathetic. What did Luis Almeda expect? To be Chairman of the Board? Chigorin believes that if illegals didn't work cheap, the fence along the border would be thirty feet high and mined on both sides. But he doesn't voice this sentiment. Instead he pulls out the bottle and offers Hector a drink, which Hector gratefully accepts.

'Lemme cut to the chase. It's the year two thousand. My father's kickin' it on the street with a bunch of his domino buddies. An argument starts, a knife comes out, a man gets killed. My father has nothin' to do with it, but he gets pulled in because the cops want him to be a witness. When he claims he didn't see anything – which he actually fucking didn't – they get right in his face. If he doesn't testify, they'll have him deported. A month later, La Migra knocks on his door. He's not home, but they come back a few weeks later, and a few weeks after that. By this time, our home is gettin' real stressed because Papi's mostly stayin' by his cousin.'

The Russian pulls to a stop at a red light. He lowers the air conditioning a notch, but doesn't speak. He knows there's a punch line coming and he doesn't want to spoil Hector's timing.

'What happened was that Papi decided to

go back to the island until the heat cooled down. Mami begged him to stay, but the man had a head of iron. Nobody could talk sense to him once he made his mind up.' Hector draws a deep breath. This is obviously hard for him. 'I drove him to the airport myself, saw him off at the American Airlines gate, hugged him goodbye. That was on the twelfth of November in two thousand and one, flight five eighty-seven. You remember, right? Flight five eighty-seven crashed in Belle Harbor a few minutes after take-off. I was twenty then, already working for the TA, and Celia had been in the military for three years. So it was Ramon who took the worst beating. He was only fifteen and he just couldn't handle it. He started runnin' with the DDP and it was all downhill from there. Mami finally kicked him out of the house after he came home one day with the gang's letters tattooed on his chest. That was two years ago.'

'The DDP? That'd do it.' The DDP is a home-grown New York street gang, its acronym standing for Dominicans Don't Play.

'See,' Hector continues, as if the Russian hadn't spoken, 'I can understand why kids

116

are attracted to the life, all that bling, rap stars treated like gods. But, man, you'd think after their dumb asses got busted a couple of times they'd figure it out. Only they don't. Or at least Ramon didn't. Every time the system cut him loose, he'd go back to sellin' powder. And I'm tellin' ya, man, Ramon never had two dimes to rub together, so what he did wasn't about money.'

Chigorin has no answer. Nor does he have the time for a philosophical exchange. They are approaching the morgue and there's one more question to be answered before he wipes the family from his list of suspects.

'You said that your mom kicked your brother out of the house. What was it, two years ago?'

'Yeah, why?'

'Well, I'm just wonderin' how come Ramon was using her apartment as his official address.'

'No big deal. Mami covered for him while he was on parole, but she couldn't let Ramon stay with her because he stole anything that wasn't nailed down. It got to the point where she didn't invite him to Christmas dinners.'

★   ★   ★

That's enough for the Russian, who never suspected the family anyway. He guides Hector through the identification process, even puts his arm around Hector's shoulder when the morgue attendant pulls down the sheet covering Ramon's face. But Chigorin's in a hurry now. During the wait before they went downstairs, he had received a phone call from his boss, Lieutenant Hamilton. The current whereabouts of a fugitive named Arvin Leopold, he told Chigorin, has been revealed by an informant and the bust is going down at 0200 hours. As Leopold's a violent felon known to carry firearms, the Russian's presence will be required.

That leaves Chigorin with just enough time to visit his main snitch, Roy 'China Boy' White. Closing in on forty, China Boy is a reformed junkie who lives in an SRO hotel, courtesy of New York's generous taxpayers. He has friends everywhere, none of whom know that he augments his meager income by selling information to the police.

Chigorin drops Hector off on Montague Street in Brooklyn Heights, then cuts back over the bridge and on to the Drive. He punches China Boy's number into his cellphone as he exits the highway at 125th

Street. The snitch answers on the second ring.

'My nigga. Wha'sup?' China Boy's voice is cheerful, as always. This is the key to his success. Everybody likes him, everybody talks to him.

'Where are ya?'

'I'm, like, indisposed.'

Chigorin knows that China Boy won't talk on the phone. He expects to be paid for his services at the time they're rendered. 'Well, you're gonna have to dispose yourself. I'm on a tight schedule.'

China Boy's voice drops to a whisper. 'Man, this woman I got is crazy mad at me. If I book, she's gonna bust a cap in my ass.'

'Ask me if I care.'

Chigorin is cruising west on 125th Street, Harlem's main drag. The sidewalks on both sides of the street are packed, the stores and shops humming right along. Harlem has gentrified somewhat, but air conditioners are still relatively uncommon and this is the fourth day of a heat wave. Inside the apartments, as Chigorin well knows, the air is stifling. The sidewalks offer the only relief, especially at night. If he were to cruise any of the residential streets, he'd find domino games on every block, lawn chairs arranged in clusters around barbecue grills, kids playing in the street, open fire hydrants, music pouring from boom boxes.

'I'm downtown,' China Boy finally says. 'On East Thirty-Eighth Street, between First and Second Avenue.'

Chigorin closes his eyes for a moment. He was just down there. 'Give me a half-hour. I'll call you when I'm on the block.'

In fact, Chigorin makes it in twenty minutes, but China Boy doesn't complain. He's outside and in the car within seconds.

'So, wha'sup?' China Boy has the narrowest eyes the Russian has ever seen. Even when he's scared, they're no more than horizontal shadows. If you didn't know the man and had to bet, you'd bet that he was blind.

'Flaco Almeda.'

China Boy's smile expands when the Russian passes him twenty dollars, the price of a consultation. 'Yeah, I knew the dawg. Flaco was a chump who thought he was bad.' China Boy slides the twenty into his pocket. 'So, you're workin' the case?'

'That's right.'

'Well, the only thing I know is that Flaco

was slingin' powder from a spot on Hamilton Place.' China Boy glances at Chigorin long enough to be sure the cop's not impressed. 'Guess you heard that,' he says.

'Flaco's got a long sheet.'

China Boy nods. He'll have to do better if he wants any more of Chigorin's hard-earned money. 'Word on the street is that Flaco was capped by the LGF. You hear what I'm sayin'? This was about territory and Flaco was in the wrong place at the wrong time.'

'You believe that?'

China Boy's story makes sense. The Mexican presence in West Harlem, once minuscule, has grown enormously over the past ten years. Mexican grocery stores are found on every block of Broadway, from 125th Street to the George Washington Bridge. That street gangs like *La Gran Familia* would accompany this transformation was inevitable.

'LGF is on the come-up in the neighborhood, no doubt about it,' China Boy explains. 'But if LGF capped Ramon, why didn't they take over the spot? Hear what I'm sayin'? 'Cause nobody's workin' that block.'

'What about Ramon? How long was he on

Hamilton Place?'

'Long time. Months, at least.'

'So, why couldn't it be a simple rip-off?'

'Yeah, that might be how it went down. Only whoever capped Ramon ain't talkin' about it. Least, not yet. But I'll keep my ears open.'

And what's that worth? Chigorin passes over a ten dollar bill. 'I want to ask you about something else.'

'Have mercy, man. I got to get upstairs.' China's Boy's hand is already on the door handle.

'This'll only take a second. You hear anything about a white man hanging out uptown? This guy is a giant, gotta be at least six-eight and built like a mountain.'

'Yeah, now you mention it. Month ago, I ran into this dude buyin' weed on Riverside Drive. Top of the line *sensemilla*. Four hundred an ounce.' China Boy chuckles. 'This is a white man you don't forget. Big, man, like the Hulk.'

'But you only saw him the one time?'

'Yeah, he wasn't no playa. Just a big cracker who wanted to score some weed.'

Chigorin takes out another ten dollar bill. 'You get his name?'

'Why, what'd he do?' The question is a ploy. Like any good businessman, China Boy's reluctant to sell his services until he knows what they're worth.

'Ten's all I got,' Chigorin states. 'And that's only for the name. And don't bullshit me. If you're makin' this up, now's the time to clear your conscience.'

Offended, China Boy stares at the Russian for a moment. Reliability is an integral part of the package he markets. He doesn't appreciate Chigorin's challenge to his word. But the Russian seems not to notice and China Boy finally continues.

'I was only with the cracker for ten minutes and we didn't have no kinda conversation, understand what I'm sayin'? He ain't none of my peeps and I don't know where to find him.'

'All I want, for now, is a name.'

'Bubba. That's what they called him when he came through the door: "Yo, Bubba, wha'sup"'

The Russian's sitting in his boss's office, intensely pleased with himself as he lays out his progress. Lieutenant Jeffrey Hamilton is obviously impressed. Hamilton's a broad-shouldered black man whose droopy expression masks a keen ambition. He'd like nothing more than to nail the subway shooter. Ramon Almeda interests him less, there being little publicity attending his demise.

'How long before you identify your suspect?' Hamilton asks.

'This guy's too big to hide, boss. Plus, I've got a street name. I'm thinkin' maybe a couple of days.'

But it's not to be. A few hours later, Hamilton leads Chigorin and five other detectives on an early morning raid. Their quarry is Arvin Leopold, whose rap sheet reveals a violent history extending back to his childhood. As they line up outside Leopold's door, the Russian's thinking that maybe they should have called in the SWAT Team. He's thinking that he's a bit long in the tooth for this kind of thing. But it's too late now. Sergeant Malkowski's already crashing a battering ram into the door just below the lock.

Chigorin charges into the apartment, gun in hand. His eyes sweep the room in search of Leopold, his focus so intense he completely overlooks Leopold's dog, a fox terrier who digs his sharp little teeth into the Russian's left ankle. Shocked by the unexpected assault, Chigorin recoils, tripping over a coffee table and slamming his head into the hardwood floor. By the time he awakens, an unresisting Leopold has been secured, the paramedics are on the way and his boss is kneeling beside him.

'Looks like you're gonna be joinin' your partner on sick leave,' Hamilton says. 'You are bleedin' like a pig.'

But Chigorin doesn't get it. His last memory is of Maureen McDonald's sweat-soaked hair whipping across the side of his face and all he can think about is how bad he needs a drink.

TEN

Hootie's awakening on the second morning of his sojourn with Bubba Yablonsky is considerably less gentle than on the first. At ten o'clock, Bubba knocks on the door, opens it and leans into room. 'Yo, Hootie, time to hit the shower. I gotta be out of here by noon.'

Hootie doesn't get it at first. He's only had four hours' sleep and his brain is still fighting the effects of last night's many indulgences. But the message finally penetrates as he completes his shower. That he'll have to leave the apartment with Bubba is a given. The only question is if they'll continue to walk the same path or go their separate ways. No more bullshit. He's going to have to choose.

The glassed-in stall has two shower heads. One pounds water on to Hootie's chest, the other on to his back. In his mom's apartment, the water in the shower jumps from hot to cold so fast that he leaves room in the tub for retreat.

Hootie steps out of the shower and drapes a thick towel across his shoulders. He raps the counter on the two-basin sink. Marble, not plastic. It's last night all over again, the ecstasy, the champagne and that girl. God, but she was fine, the finest woman he's ever had.

Hootie comes out of the bathroom to discover Bubba laying a pair of gray slacks and a polo shirt on the bed. The shirt is not new and its little alligator logo has faded to a pale green. But of course, that would be the look, downtown white casual. Can he pull it off? Hootie's nineteen years old and the ways of rich white men are known to him only through television and the movies.

'The guy who lives here, he's about your size,' Bubba says. 'I just figured you been wearin' those clothes for the last two days and they could use a rest.'

And Bubba's right about that, too. The Yankees' uniform shirt and the mid-calf shorts he's been wearing definitely need a rest, if not out and out retirement.

'I'm making breakfast,' Bubba explains as

he retreats through the door. 'See you in a few minutes.'

The clothes fit well enough, including the socks and a pair of casually-scuffed Italian loafers. On impulse, Hootie dials his sister, thinking that even the phone is a gift, that outside of his underwear, he has nothing of his own. After several rings, he gets Teesha's voicemail, but he doesn't leave a message. Instead, he examines himself in a full length mirror, thinking he could be anyone, just like Bubba said. Anyone at all.

Hootie remembers the kids at school, the ones who called him What Is It? For a time, he had to fight every day. And that brings up another question. Does Bubba think he's a punk? Even as Hootie observed its rituals, especially while he was imprisoned on Rikers Island, he always believed street macho to be actually stupid. Yeah, there were times when you had to take a stand – in Otis Bantum, punks were no more than slaves. But even the biggest, baddest dudes eventually became targets for some wannabe out to make a reputation. Eventually, they accumulated more scars than a fighting pit bull.

Hootie runs his fingers over the granite

top of the center island. He notes the prep sink at one end, the gleaming pots and pans dangling from an overhead rack, the stainless steel appliances. Cracker bling. The refrigerator's big enough to hide a sumo wrestler.

Bubba lays a cup of coffee and a sherbet glass filled with grapes, pineapple chunks, diced apples and halved-strawberries on the counter. Everything fresh, as usual. Hootie sits on one of the stools. After a minute, he asks, 'Did you cap that dealer?'

Bubba's shredding cheese in a Cuisinart, a genuine Cuisinart. He does not pause, does not even hesitate. Finally, he says, 'Every great fortune begins with a crime. You give me thirty grand, I'll turn it into three hundred. You give me three hundred, I'll turn it into three million. Just like I'm gonna turn this cheese into the best omelet you ever tasted.'

'I heard that song before, the one about the three million. From Amelia.'

'I hear what you're sayin', Hootie. For all you know, I could be taking you for a long ride down a bad road. But I don't know you, either. I'm going on pure instinct here.'

'That doesn't answer my question.'

Bubba breaks five eggs into a stainless steel bowl. He adds salt and pepper, a pinch of fresh dill and a pinch of tarragon. Finally, he begins to whisk the mixture.

'Hootie, you're pushin' me here. What happened before you came on the scene is not your problem. I shouldn't have to tell you that.'

Mind your own business. The first rule in the prison survival manual. If Hootie asks the question again, Bubba will have to react. Hootie's not about to challenge Bubba, who killed a man over an insult. But he's satisfied anyway. A convincing denial would have been easy for a scam artist like Bubba, whether he did it or not.

'Tell me what I have to do, in detail.'

'As it turns out, we're on a tighter schedule than I expected. We need to purchase equipment this afternoon and that means you walkin' into the store. It also means you when the time comes to contact the mark, and ditto if somebody has to meet the asshole face to face. Later on, if all goes well, you'll buy those Cookinarts I told you about, and you'll arrange to make the spot and buy the air time. You're going to be the face of whatever corporation we create.'

Hootie bristles. He's wondering what Bubba intends to contribute. But then he admits that Bubba's already taken the biggest risk of all. The punishment for murder is twenty-five to life.

'So, what's in it for me?'

'In the beginning, no more than room and board.' Bubba slides the whisked eggs into an omelet pan. He checks the light under the pan, then continues. 'Remember what I said about thinking outside the box? The dudes I jailed with, the horizon of their lives doesn't extend beyond the next job. They knock over a liquor store, split the money with their partners, go their separate ways. That won't happen here. We'll live where we can, buy what we have to, but most of the money goes back into the pot. I'm out to build a future, Hootie, living in the eternal present being a sure-fire recipe for spending most of your life in a cell.'

Bubba's right about one thing. The cheese omelet he serves, along with slices of onion rye bread, is the best Hootie's ever had. Hootie eats quickly, then pours himself a second cup of coffee. It's Bubba who picks up their conversation.

'You got three choices, the way I see it. You

131

can move back into the straight world, get your GED, maybe enroll in a junior college. Or you can do a few more third-rate burglaries before you get popped again. Or you can throw in with me and Amelia. We might crash and burn, I admit that, but it's not too likely when you consider the circumstances. I mean, what's the mark gonna do? Go to the cops and tell 'em, "Hey, I'm a chicken hawk and I'm being blackmailed with pictures of me screwin' a little kid"?'

Hootie knows he's supposed to laugh, but he can't. All Bubba's done here is revive Hootie's misgivings. Bubba the pimp, Amelia the whore, a pedophile free to prey on other children.

'I got problems with bein' a pimp,' he says.

'A pimp? Listen close, Hootie. The foster family Amelia grew up with? They passed her around as a party favor. Now she's got a chance to get clear and she's takin' it. And here's somethin' else you might consider. Once the mark pays off, we're gonna use a software program to blur out Amelia's face, then make a DVD and mail it to the Sex Crimes Unit. Remember, the mark's not committing a crime. Amelia's as old as you are.'

Outflanked, Hootie changes the subject. 'How do you know the mark has the money to pay off?'

'He lives in a section of Bayside, out in Queens, called Bayside Gables. His house, it's gotta be five thousand square feet. I saw the place myself. Plus, I paid a friend of a friend to check his credit report. He's triple-A, Hootie, with a credit score of eight-ten. He can put together a thirty grand pay-off with credit cards alone.'

Bubba collects the dishes and carries them into the kitchen. 'I was hopin' to give it a few more days, so we could get to know each other better. Unfortunately, the mark's heading off on an extended business trip next week. We don't hook him now, we'll have to wait a month. That's not in the budget, my man. Which means you're gonna have to make a decision.'

The sharp clack of a key turning in a lock interrupts their conversation. Amelia walks into view a moment later, her smile lighting the room. Hootie stares at that smile. He's telling himself that Amelia's smile is way too bright for a girl who was passed around as a party favor. He's telling himself maybe that foster care family resides only in Bubba's

133

imagination. Maybe there's no mark, either. Except for Judson Two-Bears Hootier.

'I'm down,' he tells Bubba. 'All the way.'

Bubba fills Hootie in as they drive through the Holland Tunnel and out to Newark. Hootie doesn't know where Bubba got the car, an ancient Crown Vic with a sun-faded hood, and he doesn't ask. The vehicle's main virtue is its size, big enough to hold Bubba whose knees bump the steering wheel even with the seat pushed all the way back. They're on their way to buy a pair of video cameras from a shop called The Crow's Nest.

'The owner's name is Larry Anderson,' Bubba explains. 'He's a real jerk, but he does high-quality miniaturization, the best around.'

Hootie's expecting a hassle when he comes through the door, but the old man with the scraggly beard seems entirely unconcerned. He barely glances at Hootie, content to produce the two items Hootie requests, a small clock in a mahogany frame and an equally small air purifier, both of which conceal a video camera.

As per Bubba's instructions, Hootie demands a demonstration, there being no time to work out any bugs. He's got three thousand dollars in his pocket and it's giving him all kinds of confidence. Though he's sure there's a surveillance camera somewhere in the store and that his face is now on it, he finds himself comfortable with his role.

The video turns out to be superb, as good as cable TV. Hootie maintains a straight face, only nodding from time to time, though he's pretty amazed. The clock and the purifier are only about six inches high and they look exactly how they're supposed to look. Like a clock and an air purifier, both working.

Satisfied, Hootie adds a final item to his order, a parabolic microphone concealed in the body of a digital camera. Then he peels twenty-seven hundred dollars off the roll and lays it on the counter. The old man's eyes light up and he doesn't even mention the sales tax.

Back in Manhattan, Hootie strolls into Washington Square at five o'clock in the afternoon. He passes beneath a massive arch honoring the first president, then cuts left to a quiet bench at the eastern edge of the park. All the action is at the western end, where a string band competes with an acrobatic troupe for the attention, not to mention the donations, of onlookers. The acrobats are the clear winners of this competition. Their leader's spiel has the crowd shaking with laughter. Which is a good thing because the troupe only has four or five moves. If they performed them one after another, the show would be over before it began.

But Hootie's not in Washington Square to observe the festivities. Amelia's to meet the mark (whose name, finally revealed to Hootie, is Sherman Cole) for the first time. The public nature of the meeting comes at Amelia's insistence. Naturally, being young and inexperienced, she's apprehensive.

Hootie slides a tiny speaker, an ear bud, into his right ear. He turns the little camera dangling from a strap around his neck until it's pointed at a bench perhaps fifty feet away. Two young women sit on the bench. Young and attractive, they lean together, co-conspirators in the adventure of New York. The shorter of the two shakes out her dreadlocks. When she speaks, her words are shockingly clear to Hootie.

'Work all week, party all weekend? It's getting tired, Karen. Bob and I might be headed for the burbs.'

Hootie turns the camera around so that the microphone lies against his chest. Great, now he can hear his heart beating, ka-boom, ka, boom, ka-boom. He takes the ear piece out, then as quickly replaces it when Amelia enters the park. She's wearing pink cotton shorts with matching sneakers and a yellow top. A pink barrette lifts a shock of her blond hair away from her scalp.

Dappled light through the leaves of an over-arching sycamore plays across Amelia's hair and shoulders as she passes from shade to sunlight. Amelia's doing her bit, looking around self-consciously, at once anxious and excited as she dodges a pair of young mothers pushing three-wheel strollers. A homeless man extends a coffee container, which he shakes as Amelia walks by. Hootie can hear the jangle of the coins and the scuffing of Amelia's sneakers. He watches her reach into the pocket of her shorts to produce a quarter, watches her drop it into the coffee container.

'God bless you, miss,' the beggar says, without looking up.

Amelia finally settles on an empty bench. She draws one foot up on the bench and runs her finger inside her sneaker. Hootie wonders what she's feeling. Is she dreading the encounter, knowing what happens next? Is she excited by the challenge? Is this merely a job?

He's hoping it's the latter, but there's no way to know. Amelia's expression doesn't change when she's approached by a man wearing khaki pants and a short-sleeved shirt. Blood-red, the shirt is imprinted with gray leaves connected by twisting vines.

'Veronica?' When Amelia doesn't respond immediately, he says, 'I'm Sherman.'

Amelia scoots over to one end of the bench. She drops her foot to the ground and tugs at the cuffs of her shorts. 'Hi,' she says.

Hootie's too far away to read Sherman Cole's expression. There's a mustache, thick eyebrows and a full head of hair that seems too uniformly dark for a man approaching forty. What's clear is that the mark's in excellent shape, the humped muscle apparent in his shoulders and back when he drops on to the bench a few feet from Amelia.

The mark begins the conversation by asking about Amelia's abusive stepfather. This is a bit of fiction that Amelia and Bubba fabricated in the weeks before the meeting. A drunk, Amelia's stepfather is quick to lash out, whether at Amelia or her chronically-depressed mom. Worse yet, twice he came into the bathroom while she was in the shower, taking advantage of a broken lock. He didn't pull back the curtain or anything. He just stood there for a moment before walking out.

The question up for discussion is whether she should say something to her mom about the two incidents. Amelia pretends to be afraid. Suppose her mom tells her step-father? That would only make things worse.

The conversation goes back and forth for a time, until Amelia looks down at her feet and says, haltingly to be sure, 'When Ernie came into the bathroom ... something happened.' A giggle, followed by a sideways glance at the mark. 'I mean, oh, my God. I didn't want to do it with him or anything. But ... but I felt excited. I felt like if he pulled back the shower curtain, I wouldn't be able to stop him.'

ELEVEN

Hootie's thinking that Amelia's aged fifteen years. He's studying her across a table located toward the back of a Greek restaurant on 7th Street. Bubba sits to Amelia's right. He's plating the appetizers, stuffed grape leaves, sautéed halloumi cheese and an artichoke moussaka. Bubba describes the dishes while he carefully assembles their plates. The patter is by now familiar to Hootie, and admittedly comforting, but he finds his attention focused on Amelia. She's no longer the perky pre-pubescent, quick with a grin or a mocking quip. Instead, her memories seem to dance in her eyes and he senses an aching, bone-deep regret in her slumped posture.

The deal is going down on the following night, in a borrowed apartment that supposedly belongs to Amelia/Veronica's older sister, now vacationing in Cape Cod. The

140

apartment is located in Kew Gardens, an upscale Queens neighborhood of single-family homes and squat brick apartment buildings, with the occasional luxury high-rise near Queens Boulevard, the main drag.

Hootie finds himself wanting to comfort Amelia. But what's can he say? I'm sorry you have to take one for the team? He slices a piece of cheese with the side of his fork and slips it into his mouth. Of course, the food is great. Of course.

Bubba commands the dinner conversation. His tone is relentlessly upbeat as he describes a must-win prison basketball game at the minimum security Menands Prison Facility. 'This was right after I was transferred down from Attica. We lost two games in a row and somehow I caught the heat, even though I played well. The deputy warden who managed us told me that my transfer papers were filled out and ready to be signed.

' "We can lose without ya," was what he said.'

The story catches Hootie's attention. Rikers Island is a rough place, but it's not like doing hard time in one of New York's maximum security prisons. First thing, the

Rikers Island complex of prisons and jails is only a short car ride from Manhattan, while the big institutions are out in the country, most of them hundreds of miles away. Hootie's mother had visited every week for the length of his incarceration, his sister almost as often. That wouldn't happen if he was upstate. If he was upstate, he'd be on his own.

'You wanna talk about motivation? Hootie, I played like a demon. I was on the court for the entire forty-eight minutes, scored thirty points and picked up twenty-two rebounds. By the time the game ended, my knees were hurting so bad I was limpin' on both legs at the same time. Meanwhile, the dep was beside himself. Over the two weeks until the next game, he was slipping me pork chop sandwiches from the warden's dining room.'

In the silence that follows, Hootie finds himself wanting to comfort Amelia as he'd comfort a child. Don't worry, it's gonna be OK. Or, worse yet: You don't have to do this, Amelia. Fortunately, he keeps his impulses under control, because when Amelia finally opens up, her misgivings have nothing to do with the sexual act.

'There's somethin' off about this scumbag,' she informs the table over cups of espresso. 'I'm talkin' about Sherman.'

'Tell me.' Bubba's anxiety is apparent. He'd skipped the encounter, sacrificing his control-freak needs to the realities at hand. Now he's paying the price.

'There's an edge to him that's just doesn't fit. Don't get me wrong, if Sherman was any hotter, he would've melted. He's a chicken hawk for sure.' She pauses long enough to swallow down a spoonful of chocolate mousse. 'Engineers are supposed to be flabby little nerds with scrawny necks and sissy handshakes. They're supposed to wear glasses and carry calculators. That's not Sherman, Bubba. Sherman's built like he spent the last ten years in a prison weight yard.'

Bubba doesn't hesitate. 'You wanna cancel, just say the word. We can always go back to one of the jerks you blew off.'

The biggest problem, from Bubba's point of view, is that the apartment they've borrowed for the day is on a side street, well away from any bar or restaurant. In a perfect world, he'd have a surveillance van equipped with hi-tech gear. Or better yet, he'd be in an adjoining apartment fully prepared to ride to the rescue. But it's not a perfect world and if Bubba wants to keep watch, he'll have to do it from the front seat of the Crown Vic, an option not in play. Like any experienced pedophile, the mark will be wary of a police sting. If he spots Bubba, he'll most likely split.

'I don't mind if the mark is a little rough,' Amelia says after a moment. 'For a lot of these guys, dominance is what it's all about. But I'm going in strapped, Bubba, so if the scumbag gets out of hand, you're gonna have to dispose of his fucking body.'

Hootie gets a look at the check before Bubba grabs it: $187.30. He watches Bubba count out the money, then add a tip generous enough to impress the surly waiter. It's nine o'clock, but their evening is far from over. Bubba drops Amelia off at the apartment, then drives Hootie to a storefront on Broadway just north of the George Washington Bridge. Wooden panels hanging from a chain behind the windows reveal the nature of the business:

ENVIOS DE DINEROS
DOCUMENTOS
IMMIGRACIÖN
ABOGADOS

One stop shopping for immigrants, legal and illegal. Send money home, acquire documents, retain a lawyer to fight La Migra.

As they come through the door, Bubba's greeted by a Latino with a pair of teardrops tattooed beneath his left eye. He clasps Bubba's hand and they bump chests, two refugees from the institution, then fixes Hootie with a hard look. The look's a matter of habit and not meant as a threat, but the implications aren't lost on Hootie. There are people in this world, one glance and you know they're not to be fucked with. Another lesson from the Rikers Island School of Hard Knocks.

Ninety minutes later, Judson Hootier has a new identity, an identity he can verify with a driver's license, a social security card and Department of Buildings ID that bears his photo. Hootie examines the driver's license under intense light, comparing it to Bubba's legit license. After a long look, he decides that the document will pass muster, though the blue on the state seal is a bit off. He is now a twenty-five-year-old Filipino named Judson Binay.

On the way home, Bubba asks Hootie about the mark. He wants to know if Hootie found the man to be menacing.

'Amelia's was right about one thing,' Hootie replies after a moment. 'The guy's fit. But so what? Where is it written that an engineer has to be soft?'

'What about his voice? You were listenin', right?'

Hootie shrugs. 'What could I say? The dude made all the right noises, especially when he was bein' sympathetic. Like he knew what he wanted and how to get it. Like he's done this before. But the alarm bells didn't ring. I'm talkin' about the ones your buddy set off a few minutes ago.'

'Fernando? He's a pussycat.' Bubba grins, then quickly becomes serious. 'What about suspicion? Did he sound suspicious?'

'Suspicious? Not that I remember.'

'See, that's what bothers me. Sherman Cole, if he gets busted, his life is over. The job, the house, the wife, the kids ... I'm talkin' about everything. So why isn't he worried about a sting? Especially if he's done this before and he knows the risks?'

The answer, to Hootie, is simple enough. 'Because Amelia looks like a kid, Bubba. In case you forgot. The cops wouldn't use a kid.'

'Yeah, you're right. They wouldn't. Plus, there's tons of evidence on Amelia's computer that can be traced back to him, not to mention the phone calls. There's nothing the asshole can do and I gotta stop worryin', right? But I still wish I could've seen him.'

Later, in the early hours of the morning, Hootie slowly awakens from a dream. A dream about dreams. He's in the massive dining room at Otis Bantum, he and his mentor, Eli Scannon, and a battle is under way. Two Latino gangs, one Dominican, the other Puerto Rican, are settling a score. Shanks flash, clubs fly, chairs smash unprotected skulls. The air is filled with tear gas and pepper spray and the curses of guards and inmates. Hootie and Eli wander through this mêlée, calm and indifferent. They breathe in the gas and the spray with no apparent discomfort.

147

'The white man's dream,' Eli tells Hootie, 'is the black man's opiate. Like religion is the opiate of the people. The black man doesn't even know these dreams are dreams. He thinks they're real, and that if he could only wake up one morning with white skin, they'd be his. I knew a woman once, liked to lie on her back and look up at the sky. Claimed she could read the future in the clouds.'

There's blood now, blood everywhere, and the cries of the wounded surround them. But Eli is oblivious. He laughs softly and says, 'There was time when I believed her. Swear to God, I was crazy in love with that gal.'

'What was her name?'

'Amelia.' Scannon lays a hand on Hootie's shoulder, bringing him to a stop. 'Amelia lived way up in the clouds, as far from the Earth as she could get. And what I'm sayin' is that I don't hold it against her. A girl comes up as hard as Amelia, she's got to dream. If it wasn't for them clouds, she wouldn't have nothin' at all.'

As Hootie's eyes finally open, Scannon's voice instantly disappears, replaced by Bubba's: 'All great fortunes,' he explains, 'begin with a crime.'

And Judson Two-Bears Hootier will no longer be a frightened nineteen-year-old, lost somewhere between boy and man, no longer be futureless, no longer be hopeless.

Hootie gets out of bed and walks to the window. He parts the curtain and looks across a chain-link fence at the back of a six-story tenement. It's four o'clock in the morning and only a single window is lit, a kitchen window. Hootie can see a woman through the window, sitting at a table. The woman is white and elderly and she leans forward, running her finger across the page of a book. Wispy tendrils of gray hair dangle in front of her face and a liquor bottle off to her left glistens.

Hootie's brain opens up a bit as he turns away. The conversation with Eli Scannon, real as it seemed, never happened. Not so for the riot, a battle between the Latin Kings and *Los Trinitarinos*. Hootie hadn't known what they were fighting about, only that it wasn't any of his business. Like most of the other prisoners in the dining room, he'd instinctively moved to the furthest wall as a Quick Reaction Squad pounded the rioters with steel batons. Unfortunately, that wasn't far enough to escape the gas and the pepper spray. By the time Hootie was escorted back to his housing area, he was coughing blood.

Hootie returns to the bed. He lies down on his back and lets his head fall to the pillow. The black man's dreams and the white man's schemes. Salt and pepper. Or pepper and salt. Many of Hootie's doubts were erased when the mark made his appearance. The man was a baby raper, no doubt about it, so hot he was on fire. That means the deal's going down. Twenty-four hours from now, they'll be in Amelia's room, burning a $30,000 DVD. And worth every nickel, surely, to Mr. Sherman Cole of Bayside Gables?

$30,000 equals $300,000 equals $3,000,000? Dream, Hootie, dream.

Hootie fishes out his new ID and examines the name and the photo. Then he looks at himself in the mirror on the bureau, moving closer until the image in the glass is confined to his head and shoulders. He's thinking that his past is behind him, that he can be anybody, anybody at all. He's thinking it's easy to be anybody when all your life you've been nobody.

TWELVE

The studio apartment they enter at eleven o'clock on the following morning is perfect. The mismatched furniture is straight out of IKEA, a blue table, a green double-dresser, a wood-frame couch bearing maroon cushions, a tweed area rug. Amelia/Veronica's sister is supposed to be a recent college graduate and there's not a single item in the entire apartment that doesn't fit.

Bubba carefully places the two surveillance cameras. The clock goes on top of a small bookcase, positioned to cover the double bed. The air purifier goes on a nightstand tucked into a corner. This camera will cover the rest of the single room, including the front door.

When Hootie plugs the air purifier into a wall socket, it hums away, the sound oddly contented, almost a purr. Amelia has kept her promise. She has a gun in her bag, a .32

caliber automatic. The weapon holds only five rounds and appears small enough to be a toy, but Hootie's not fooled. He knows the most important factor isn't the size of the gun, but the intentions of the lady holding it. Amelia's eyes seem harder today and she's no longer projecting doubt. Her bag will be on the floor next to the bed where she can get to it in a hurry.

Hootie's relaxed about his role in the day's events, which as far as he can tell comes to exactly nothing. He's thinking about the Asian girl in the club. He wants more of that life and screw the risk and fuck the straight world. There's a felony on his record now, so he can forget about career choices like New York's bloated civil service. As far as New York's concerned, he's not fit to sling garbage. So, what's his fate? By dint of hard work and due diligence? Shuffling boxes in a warehouse for ten dollars an hour, no health insurance, no pension? Not to mention never being able to support a family?

Outside, the clouds are bunching together, growing darker as they get closer to the earth. The heatwave is about to crack wide open. Hootie watches the process while Amelia calls the mark. He listens to her slow tease. Yes, she's at her sister's apartment in Queens ... But no, she's not quite ready to give him the address. There's talk of the Playboy Channel and Internet pornography (Amelia/Veronica's fascinated by pornography) and how experience matters. But still, but still...

Bubba's in the kitchen when Amelia hangs up. He's found a cache of takeout menus stashed behind the microwave. After some debate, they order in a pizza and a six-pack of Cokes from an Italian restaurant that boasts a coal-fired oven. Hootie doesn't care for the pizza – not enough cheese – but he manages to eat a couple of slices, as he manages to feign interest when Bubba tunes the little television set to a Yankees game. Hootie's never liked baseball.

The first thunderstorm explodes over New York just after two o'clock, the clouds spitting rapid-fire bolts of lightning. At the Stadium, the grounds crew rushes to cover the field while the fans beat a hasty retreat. Bubba watches the action from the apartment's single armchair. He sits with his hands folded across his chest, his thin lips compressed. For once, there's no pep talk. Amelia lies on the bed, staring up at the ceiling, her thoughts her own. The rain is loud enough to drown conversation anyway, slapping against the windows like a swarm of invading insects.

Bubba reaches out to adjust the volume. With no end to the rain in sight, the YES channel has switched to a biography of Lou Gehrig, the Yankees legendary first baseman. Hootie is drawn into the story despite himself. One of the greatest hitters to ever play the game, Gehrig was at the height of his career when he was struck with the illness that came to bear his name. In 1937, he batted .351. In 1938, he could barely field his position. In 1941, he was buried.

Hootie's fascinated by the rapid fall, the man who had everything reduced to a paralysed husk in a wheelchair. As he watches the funeral, he recalls an Eli Scannon lecture on the black man's superstitions. Borne by events as unpredictable as they are malevolent, disaster comes to the black man as a random act. Any place can be the wrong place, any time the wrong time. This is a natural outgrowth of the Jim Crow era. Find a white woman murdered and every black man within a hundred miles was at risk.

'I'm gonna call,' Amelia finally says.

'It's early.' Bubba shuts down the TV. 'Plus, if he wants to get here, he's gonna have to take a boat.'

Amelia grins. 'Maybe I wanna test his devotion, find out if he really loves me. I mean, if hail and rain can't stop a mailman ... Anyway, it's four o'clock now and I'm gonna tell him that I have to be home at nine. That means I have to leave at eight, which means he has to leave at seven thirty so I can straighten up the apartment. I should call you with an all-clear by a quarter to eight.'

Bubba stands up and thrusts his hands into his pockets. He's not happy and Hootie knows why. They'll have to confront the storm and the car is parked two blocks away. Bubba doesn't argue, though. He rummages in a closet and comes up with a folding umbrella, one of those five-dollar jobs sold by street pedlars. Hootie thinks it'll function for maybe ten seconds before turning inside out.

'Alright, go ahead,' Bubba tells Amelia.

The conversation this time is marked by long silences at Amelia's end. Timidity is the order of the day, a young girl drawn in two directions, frightened and excited at the same time. Amelia finally tells the mark that if he comes over, he'll have to leave at seven thirty, '...because if I'm not home by nine, my father will kill me, OK?'

Hootie doesn't have to hear the other side of the conversation. He knows that Sherman's yessing away. Anything she wants, however she wants it. Or even if she doesn't want it. Toward the end of the conversation, just before surrendering the address, Amelia asks, 'If ... if, like, nothing happens ... would that be alright?'

Bubba's standing by the window, his attention focused on Amelia. Outside, the wind has dissipated somewhat, though it continues to pour. Hootie drinks in the scene. Now that he's gotten past his instinctive distaste, he finds himself admiring his new partners. Amelia's performance is without a false note, as it was on the prior evening in Washington Square.

Hootie imagines Bubba passing the entire ten years of his sentence preparing for the day he got out. Always positive, always making the best of his situation, always hustling. Which is not to say that he isn't crazy. That business with the rat was about as crazy as it gets.

'You ready?' Bubba asks.

Though Hootie's not sure who's being asked the question, he heads for the kitchen where he finds a large garbage bag. He cuts holes in the bag for his head and his arms, creating a poor man's poncho. He's wondering what to say to Amelia, finally deciding to let Bubba do the talking.

'You up for this?' Bubba's small gray eyes are as penetrating as Hootie has ever seen them.

Amelia raises a steady hand. She cocks her head to one side and winks. 'Get outta here, the both of ya.'

Bubba's not finished, though. He wags a finger as he lectures. 'You get in trouble and don't feel like shooting the prick, hit the speed dial on your cellphone. I won't be more than five minutes away, promise.'

Hootie's improvised poncho is of no more value than Bubba's umbrella. Both men are soaked before they reach the end of the first block. Hootie wants to make a dash for it. Not so Bubba. He's got the little umbrella wrapped around his head like a turban and he's looking down at the sidewalk, his long stride deliberate. When they finally reach the car, he stands for a moment with the keys in his hand, looking back toward the apartment where Amelia waits.

'Alright, let's go,' he finally says, sounding as though he just made up his mind.

They drive along Queens Boulevard through slackening rain, from Hillside Avenue to Continental Avenue and back again, at no time more than a few miles from the apartment. Amelia's not expected to call for another four hours and Bubba's too keyed up to sit in a parked car. Or to remain silent.

'You ever see the commercial for the Stick-Up Light?' he asks.

Hootie pulls his wet shirt away from his skin as he rummages around in his brain. Finally, he says, 'Yeah, maybe. That's the one you're supposed to put it in a closet.'

'That's it. A fluorescent light that works off a battery. You stick it up on the wall, pull the little chain and you have a light for those dark corners. Even comes with a holder so you can slide the unit out and take it wherever you want.'

'OK, so what?'

'Well, the guy who invented the light, man named Paul Belvedere, started out doin'' low-end infomercials in Mississippi. That was all he could afford, even though he begged and borrowed from everyone he knew. You hear what I'm sayin'? This was a one-shot deal, Hootie. If he didn't move every single unit, his entrepreneurial life was over. But he did move them. He sold out and shifted his advertising to a regional market in the south-east, then to the big nationals, CNN, FOX – even the networks. Finally, he sold the patent to a manufacturer for ten million dollars. Now you can find a Stick-Up Light in every little drug store. Or you can buy one online at hundreds of websites.'

Hootie stares through the windshield. The clouds are pulling away, the sky rising. The rain has all but stopped and a stiff breeze rattles the parking signs along the curb.

'You an inventor, too?' he asks.

'No, you're missing the point. You hear about the guys who started Google, how much money they made?'

'Sure.'

'Well, that way's not open to us. We don't have the knowledge and we never will. So the point I'm makin is that there's another way. Paul Belvedere was drivin' a truck when he started out. If he can do it, we can do it. All it takes is will.'

They drive for another half-hour before Bubba runs out of will and decides to park the car. They've got the heater turned up high, with the hot air blowing out through the vents and on to their wet clothing. Hootie thinks he's sweating fast enough to replace the moisture in his shirt before it evaporates.

Bubba turns off Queen Boulevard on to 82nd Avenue. Parking spaces are at a premium in Kew Gardens and residents commonly pay three hundred dollars a month for a space in an underground garage. Bubba doesn't expect to find a legal parking place and he's not disappointed. He pulls up next to an SUV the size of a tank and prepares to back into the curb beside a fire hydrant. As long as they don't leave the car, they can stay here as long as they want.

Which doesn't turn out to be very long at all. Bubba's cellphone goes off as he shifts the transmission into park, projecting a tuneless rendition of a Mary Blige tune. He yanks it from his shirt pocket, glances at the caller ID screen and presses the 'on' button. The faint voice on the other end of the call belongs to a man and it comes from a distance.

'You made a big mistake,' the voice says, 'and now you gotta pay for it.'

Bubba comes out of the space fast, in the process managing to crack into both cars, front and rear. He tears up to the corner, then gets himself trapped on a one-way street running away from the apartment. Hootie's heart is now in his throat and it's pounding away at his Adam's apple. He can see that Bubba's scared, but other than a murmured 'holy shit', Bubba's chosen not to explain. So maybe it's not happening, maybe it's not a false alarm, maybe when they enter the apartment, they'll find the mark happily engaged in the activity he came for. In that case, the shakedown will just have to start a little early. No big deal, right?

The trip takes less than ten minutes, with Bubba running a pair of lights, but they're too late, nevertheless. The apartment is empty, the two cameras and Amelia's bag gone as well. Hootie's head swivels back and forth, a metronome, as he fights to maintain some minor semblance of outward calm. This is dread, this is the monster in the closet, the one his mother told him didn't exist. This is every nightmare suddenly proven real.

'There's blood over here.'

Bubba's voice pierces Hootie's thoughts, slicing them neatly in two. If there was ever a time for doing and not thinking, this is it. Hootie walks over to Bubba and examines the drops of blood on the wall and floor. The blood is fresh and shockingly red, but there isn't a lot of it.

'I gotta clean this up,' Bubba says.

'What are you talkin' about? We have to find Amelia.'

Bubba heads for the sink. He wets a sponge, tears off a fistful of paper towels and returns to the bloodstains. The blood on the floor comes up easily, but the blood on the wall smears. Bubba continues to scrub until the stain is barely visible, then shoves the paper napkins and the sponge into a plastic bag before heading out the door. Hootie stares at the expanse of Bubba's shoulders and back, trailing him out to the street where Bubba dumps the bag in a garbage can. Then they're in the car and Bubba's moving through and around the traffic on Queens Boulevard.

'We're goin' back to the apartment. I got a piece stashed in my bureau.' Bubba pauses, though he doesn't look at Hootie. Then he says, 'You wanna bail, Hootie, I won't hold it against you.'

Hootie bites at his lower lip. He's thinking Bubba's right. What he should do is yell, 'Stop the car and let me the fuck out.'

'Then what?' he finally asks. 'After you get the gun?'

'You serious? I know where the jerk lives, Hootie.'

'The jerk? Funny you should use that word, because the only jerks I know are sittin' right in this car.'

Bubba turns on to the Grand Central Parkway and heads north toward the Triborough Bridge. He's running about ten miles an hour above the speed limit, his eyes focused on the road, the top of his head brushing the roof liner. He doesn't speak or seem about to speak, and Hootie finally becomes rattled.

'Killing Sherman won't bring Amelia back,' he says.

Bubba laughs. 'Kill Sherman? Hootie, I'm gonna kill his wife and his kids. I'm gonna kill his fuckin' dog.'

Hootie settles back against the seat. He's wondering exactly what he owes these two crackers? Eli Scannon would laugh in his face, damsels in distress not being relevant to the black man's experience, especially if they're white damsels. But Hootie knows something else, something he doesn't think Eli would understand. The minute he's alone, he's gonna start thinkin' about Amelia, about what might be happening to her. This is not a road he's anxious to travel.

What Hootie does, finally, is hesitate for too long. He absorbs this fact as he and Bubba approach the building where he, Bubba and Amelia have been living. Four cops step away from the door to block the sidewalk. Three of the cops are in uniform, the fourth wears a rumpled suit and has a thick bandage on the back of his head. Hootie feels Bubba lurch against him, feels something slide down into his pocket, a set of keys that clink softly against the coins at the bottom.

'Do what you have to do,' Bubba tells him. 'Find Amelia.'

Hootie swallows his response. Bubba's already gone, striding ahead, shoulders squared, finger curled into his palms.

Hootie finds himself glad he's not on the receiving end of Bubba's determination, but the cops are less impressed. With them it's more like 'been there, done that'. They let Bubba come to within ten feet before one of the uniformed cops produces a Taser. He doesn't say 'Stop right there' or 'Put your hands up' or 'Get down on your face'. No, he pulls the trigger and reduces Bubba Yablonsky to a twitching pile of meat on the sidewalk.

Hootie observes Bubba's demise without moving so much as an inch. Fighting cops is not a game you can win. He's standing with his hands above his head, watching the detective in the suit limp toward him. The detective's small gray eyes are shadowed by an over-arching brow, but Hootie can read them well enough. To the man behind those eyes, Judson Hootier is no more human than a cockroach on the station house wall.

'Hi,' the cop says, 'I'm Detective Chigorin. How ya doin?'

THIRTEEN

By Wednesday morning, a day after he cracks his skull, the Russian's had enough. He tells the docs if they don't sign him out of the hospital, say within the next hour, he'll walk out on his own. The doctor in charge states the facts as she understands them, and not for the first time. Chigorin has suffered a fairly severe concussion, with some internal bleeding. Caution demands that he be monitored for another twenty-four hours. Plus, he needs to stay off his dog-bitten ankle, which is inflamed and threatening to become infected.

Chigorin simply repeats the message: 'One hour.'

Forty-five minutes later, as he's hopping into a wheelchair, one of the hospital's many residents, a doc he recognizes but can't name, hands him a prescription for antibiotics.

'You want to keep a close eye on that head injury. If it goes bad, you'll need to find an emergency room in a hurry.'

'Goes bad like how?'

'Like if renewed bleeding should put enough pressure on your brain to cause sudden, irreversible death.'

Chigorin stares at the doc for a minute. He's thinking, Fuck it, if I don't have a drink soon I'll die anyway. As the aide pushes the chair down the hall, Chigorin turns and waves. 'See ya, Doc.'

'Fine, Detective,' the resident calls after him, 'but whatever you do, don't drink.'

Outside, Chigorin hails a passing gypsy cab and rides it to the precinct, where he checks in with his boss, Lieutenant Hamilton. The lieutenant assures the Russian that his injury is line-of-duty in nature.

'Most likely, if you wanna go the way of your partner, you could milk your sick leave for the next six months.'

Throughout the conversation, Lieutenant Hamilton projects the concern of a father for a sick child. Not so Chigorin's peers in the squad room. To be taken down by a raging pit bull is an acceptable excuse for sustaining an injury. But not a ten-pound fox terrier.

'That's the whole point,' Chigorin attempts to explain. 'The mutt was so small I didn't notice him until he sunk his teeth into my ankle.'

The Russian's remark is greeted by a wave of laughter that follows him as he limps to his car and the bottle stored under the seat. He takes a long swig, then settles back to let the alcohol works its way through his body. The Russian imagines he can hear a breathy little pop as his neurons switch from off to on, and not only in his befogged brain. He can feel the juice in his toes, in his eyes. Even his teeth seem more awake.

Chigorin stashes the bottle and points the car toward Anselm's. As he crosses the Triborough Bridge, he finds himself thinking about the giant called Bubba. The Russian's stay in the hospital wasn't entirely unproductive. The cartridge casing recovered from the subway platform was finally compared to the casings found at the Almeda homicide scene. According to Ballistics, the resulting match is definitive – the nine millimeter handgun that killed Flaco was also used to cap the rat. The only question is what Chigorin wants to do about it, if anything.

There's only a single customer in Anselm's when the Russian walks inside and it's not, as Chigorin was hoping, Maureen Mc-Donald. But Nat Cudlow is a fellow sailor of the alcohol seas, which is some comfort, though he and Chigorin are far from friends. Nat's way too guilt-ridden, one of those drunks who believes he's let his family and his country down, that he's beyond redemption, that every drop he drinks hammers another nail into the flesh of his Savior. Chigorin, by contrast, isn't given to self recrimination. He doesn't blame anybody for his addiction, least of all himself.

Anselm walks up to the bar, bottle in hand, as Chigorin sits down. 'Have ya been wounded?' he asks. Unlike the Russian's fellow detectives, Anselm's tone is solicitous.

'Took a shot from behind,' the Russian explains. 'Never saw it coming.'

'And your limp?'

'Twisted my ankle on the way down. It's nothing.'

Chigorin finishes his first drink, then orders lunch from the Lucky Star, a Chinese takeout joint a few blocks away. Wonton soup and crispy shredded beef. He requests that the beef dish be spicy and the man taking the order dutifully repeats his request. But when his order arrives a few minutes later, the dish is still bland, as he knew it would be.

Anselm draws a small draft and steps to the bar. He sips at the beer, then says, to Nat Cudlow as well as Chigorin, 'Did ya hear about Father Ansparger?'

Cudlow groans. 'If this is another altar boy story, I don't wanna hear it. My faith's stretched thin enough already.'

'Sorry to disappoint you, lad, but the priest wasn't after the altar boys. It seems the good father's decided to marry. Last night he turned in his cassock and his collar.'

'I'll drink to that,' the Russian announces.

The discussion that follows is about College Point and St. Ann's, the church they wish they attended more regularly. It's about community and all present find it comforting. They don't condemn the priest – far from it. To a man, they're of the opinion that celibacy lies at the bottom of the gay-priest scandals. A man who lives without sexual relationships in the real world is automatically suspected of being a homosexual. Not so a priest, which is why the priesthood turned into a romping ground for pedophiles.

'Are rabbis somehow less holy for having carnal knowledge?' Chigorin asks. 'Are Protestant ministers?'

Chigorin's questions are answered by his cellphone, which begins to vibrate in his pocket. He places a hand on the bandage covering the back of his head. The pain's been dulled by alcohol, but it's still there. Also the pain in his ankle. He has every excuse not to answer. Half his snitches have the number and he's on sick leave.

When the phone stops vibrating, the Russian slides it out of his pocket and checks the caller ID: PRIVATE NAME/ PRIVATE NUMBER. He accesses his voicemail, but there's nothing there. Finally, he presses the redial button. That's another thing about the Russian. He's gotta know.

'Wha'sup?'

Chigorin sighs into the phone. It's China Boy White. 'You called me,' the Russian says.

''At's right. I got the dirty on that Bubba dude you're lookin' for.'

'So, what is it?'

China Boy laughs into the phone. 'Money talks, my man. Bullshit walks.'

'Hey, I'm off-duty and way out in Queens. Maybe I could tighten you up next time I see ya.'

'Be serious, man. You don't want the information, there's others who will.'

Impatient, Chigorin slides off his stool, his ankle screaming in protest. 'Look here, China Boy, this better be good. Because I'm in no mood to drag my ass into Manhattan for a line of crap.'

'Crap? Detective, I'm talkin' headlines here. Crime of the motherfuckin' century. What I got is filthy.'

Chigorin arranges to meet China Boy in an hour at the corner of 96th and Second. He hangs up and shoves the phone in his pocket. China Boy is prone to exaggeration, so the crime of the century bit can pretty much be discounted. Still...

'What was that about?' Cudlow asks.

'About a giant white guy named Bubba who may have killed a coke dealer named Almeda.'

'Bubba Yablonsky?'

Chigorin freezes. 'Say what?'

'Played center for St. John's about ten years ago. That's my Alma Mater. He killed one of his teammates, beat him to death.'

'I remember the incident, now you mention it,' Anselm declares. 'He was convicted, right?'

'Pled guilty to manslaughter. Sentenced to ten years.'

Chigorin interrupts. 'You have a computer here?' he asks Anselm.

'In the back.' The bartender's voice reveals a defensive note. For working men of his generation, Chigorin's too, computers are generally reserved for the less than manly. 'I use it to place orders.'

The Russian limps off toward Anselm's tiny office, Anselm and Cudlow following behind. Five minutes later, a Google search leads to a *Daily News* article: Conrad 'Bubba' Yablonsky was paroled from the Menands Correctional Facility on June 14th, six weeks before.

Chigorin taps his wallet, thinking the information would've cost him a c-note if he'd had to buy it from China Boy. He limps back to his bar stool and hoists himself up. Now what? He drains his glass and signals for another. Beside him, Cudlow describes

Bubba Yablonsky's prowess on a basketball court.

The Russian listens with one ear while he considers his options. He should, he knows, report the information to Detective Nick Campo, who's inherited the case. But Campo's a moron, a blunt object whose bullying interrogations drive suspects into a shell more often then they produce results. And that's especially true of seasoned convicts like Bubba Yablonsky.

Still, why should he care? Almeda was a drug dealer, his death little more than an occupational hazard. If Campo fucks up the investigation and the murder isn't cleared, the world as we know it will not come to an end. No, the heavens do not cry out for justice and he's not the Lone fuckin' Ranger.

Chigorin backs up a bit. He lets his eyes roam over the bar's generic interior: the mirror behind Anselm, the booze stacked before the mirror, the sinks, the beer taps, the worn wooden floors, the tin ceiling, the rickety tables. Anselm's claim to individuality rests entirely on its paneled walls and the messages carved into them, floor to ceiling. Encouraged by three generations of

Deenihans, a ban on obscenity is the only restriction imposed.

The Russian has taken his turn here, carving his name and the name of a long vanished girlfriend. His inscription is typically insipid – a name, a date, a commitment to eternal devotion – yet there are a few messages that reach out for attention.

The fourth floor is a hell-hole deserted by the Lord.

If the angels cared/Who among us would be spared?

My family is a living argument for euthanasia.

There is no life without community – the hermit suffers the worst fate of all.

Chigorin's big on community, some might even say desperate, especially since his divorce. Even at the time, when his state of denial approached the absolute, he'd dimly realized that having a family placed him in the great community of married men. And thus his banishment – for good reasons, it has to be admitted – carried dual consequences, a loss of family and community both. So yes, he's been reduced, his connections to the world grown more tenuous. Worse still, he knows he'll never make it right and he doesn't want to. He's content with the identities he has left, bar fly and cop.

'Hang on a second,' Chigorin tells Cudlow, bringing him to a halt in mid-sentence. He takes out his cellphone and his PDA.

'What are you gonna do?' Anselm asks. Like Cudlow, he's thrilled to be part of a celebrity investigation.

'Call Bubba's parole officer, get his current address. Then I'll see.'

FOURTEEN

Chigorin stuffs the last bit of a jelly doughnut into his mouth. He chews thoughtfully for a moment, then chases the doughnut with the dregs of his third cup of coffee. Chigorin's in the squad room of the Sixth Precinct, staring at Bubba Yablonsky through a one-way mirror. The giant's sitting behind a small table made even smaller by his immense size. He seems relaxed, though Chigorin's sure his guts are churning. Well, credit where credit is due. Bubba's been all by his lonesome for almost two hours. Most other mutts would either be asleep or climbing the wall.

The Russian crosses the squad room, weaving between battered desks that seem almost randomly placed. He looks in through a second mirror, this time at Skinny Kid, the boy in the video taken at the subway station. The boy's driver's license identifies him as Judson Binay, age twenty-five, but the license is phoney and Chigorin assumes that Judson Binay is an alias. Though Chigorin might uncover the boy's true identity by fingerprinting him, he's decided to convince the kid to identify himself.

Unlike his partner, Judson Binay's not cuffed, neither his wrists nor his ankles. And also unlike his partner, Skinny Kid's nerves are on full display. He's pacing the tiny room, three strides forward, three strides back. Like he's thinking there's some place he has to be, like he knows he's not going anywhere, like he can't reconcile the two. Par for the course.

Chigorin laughs to himself as he heads off to the bathroom. When he saw Skinny Kid and Bubba get out of the car, he experienced a joy that bordered on rapture. He felt as he had all those years ago when he made his first Holy Communion. He felt almost transformed.

Talk about luck. The little jerk can put the gun that killed Almeda in Bubba's hand. He's a gift from above, from St. Michael, slayer of dragons and patron of villain-hunting cops.

'Hey, Chigorin, how long are you gonna let 'em stew?' The question is posed by Sergeant Ed Vincenzo, the Sixth Precinct's squad commander. The Russian's use of the Sixth Precinct is a courtesy necessarily limited by the squad's own needs. Right now it's quiet, with all but one of Vincenzo's detectives in the field.

'Let me hit the bathroom, Sarge, and I'm on it.'

Inside a stall, Chigorin fortifies himself for the battle ahead. He takes a generous swig of the vodka in his flask, then chomps down on a wintergreen tic tac. The vodka meshes nicely with the caffeine and sugar already in his system. He's as ready as he's ever going to be.

Bubba doesn't look up when Chigorin walks into the room, nor does he acknowledge the Coke and the doughnut the cop lays on the table between them. Last time out, in an attempt to avoid arrest with a claim of self-defense, he'd cooperated with the detectives. His reward was ten years in prison.

'Don't waste your breath,' he says. 'I have the right to remain silent and I'm takin' it.'

'Hey, did I accuse you of somethin'?'

'I have the right to remain silent,' Bubba repeats, 'and I'm takin' it.'

'OK, Bubba, if that's the way you wanna go. But I got one question anyway, which you don't have to answer. Did you really expect that punk kid to stand up? Did you think he wouldn't put the gun in your hand? I'm talkin' about the one that killed Flaco Almeda. And while we're on the subject, whatta ya think I've been doin' for the past two hours?'

The Russian's pregnant pause is met by silence – Bubba still hasn't looked up – and the cop's the first to speak. 'You're pissed off about getting' tased. I can understand your point, but—'

'I'm pissed off because you're shitting all over my constitutional rights.'

Chigorin's not impressed by the righteous tone. Bubba's been here before and he should know better. 'True enough, Yablonsky, but the ref's not payin' attention, is he?'

Bubba finally raises his head to stare directly into Chigorin's eyes. His hands curl into fists and he presses them against his chest. 'Take your questions and shove 'em up your mother's ass. I'm not talkin' to ya.'

One thing about the Russian, he knows when he's not wanted. Still, as he opens the door, he offers a piece of advice. 'Ya know, you really oughta watch what you say about people's mothers. A lotta cops, they're not as good-natured as me.'

Not for a moment does the Russian consider his retreat an acknowledgement of Bubba Yablonsky's rights. Later on, depending on what he gets from Skinny Kid, he'll probably take another shot at Bubba. In his opinion, rights are beautiful things, proof being that accused cops are quick to assert them. But he wasn't joking around when he said that nobody was looking. And Bubba didn't laugh, either.

Despite his youth, Hootie's not naïve about cops. Far from it. He's even aware of the part of the Miranda warning that goes 'anything you say can be used against you'. But he can't stop thinking about Amelia, can't stop thinking that he has to get out of here, even though he doesn't have any idea what he'll do next. He feels like he's in a dream, opening doors, stepping into rooms that turn out to be the same room he left. That changes abruptly when the wounded cop makes his entry. Now he's just scared.

'Hi,' the cop says, 'I'm Detective Chigorin. In case you forgot.'

Hootie stares at the bandage on the Russian's head. 'I want to know what I'm here for. I have a right to know.'

Chigorin shakes his head. 'The first thing you're gonna do is sit down.' He points to the chair behind the table, the one against the wall. 'In the hump seat.'

The Russian waits until Hootie complies, then says, 'Now, can I get you something? A Coke maybe? Or if you need to hit the john, this would be a good time.'

Hootie wants to maintain a defiant attitude, but his bladder is indeed full. And he's thirsty, too. 'The bathroom,' he says.

Chigorin opens the door, waits for Hootie to pass before him. He points to the men's room. 'There ya go,' he says. 'I'll meet you back here.'

When Hootie returns, there's a can of Coke sitting on the table. He pops the tab and drinks. The cop's failure to accompany him to the bathroom caught him by surprise. Does it mean he's not a suspect? Or does the cop think he's too much of a punk to attempt an escape?

'Ya know,' the cop says, 'what I'm supposed to do now is explain your constitutional rights. The only problem is I don't know who you are.'

'Judson Binay,' Hootie says.

Chigorin eases himself into the chair opposite Hootie. He leans forward to gingerly probe the swelling around his ankle. 'I got bit by a dog, a tiny little dog, if you could believe that. The fuckin' mutt had teeth like needles.'

The room they occupy is smaller than a prison cell. Wood table and chairs, tiled floor, dirty brown walls, dirty white ceiling, dirty mirror. Hootie feels the trap closing.

'Are you gonna tell me why I'm here?' he asks.

'No, I'm not. Not until you identify yourself. That driver's license in your pocket? It's bogus, my man, completely bogus.'

'Only the age,' Hootie claims. 'So I can drink in bars.'

'So you can drink in bars? Let me see if I've got this right. You're saying that if I run your prints, they'll come back Judson Binay? That's what you're tellin' me?' Chigorin's narrow lips expand into a humorless smile. 'By the way, what are you? I mean what nationality?'

Hootie ignores the question. 'You have no cause to fingerprint me. I haven't committed any crime.'

'You need to face the facts, kid. You're not getting' out of here until you're properly identified.'

Hootie watches the cop settle back in his chair. This is not Hootie's first time in the box and he knows that silence is a technique cops employ to get suspects talking. He knows, too, that if he resists, the cop will definitely run his prints. Another humiliation.

'My name's Judson Hootier,' Hootie admits.

'You have a street name, an alias?'

'Hootie.'

The Russian nods. 'How old are you?'

'Nineteen.'

'Are you on parole?'

Hootie shakes his head. 'I haven't committed any crime,' he insists. 'This ain't right.'

'Just answer the question.'

'I'm on probation.'

'For what offense?'

'Burglary.'

'You do any time?'

'Nine months. On Rikers.'

'When did you get out?'

The question stops Hootie in his tracks. It seems like a million years since he stepped on to a DOC bus for the ride to Queens Plaza. Without warning, Bubba's voice sounds in his ears. *Every great fortune begins with a crime.* That was wrong and he should have recognized the problem right away. Maybe every great fortune does begin with a crime, but it has to be an unpunished crime.

'Ten days ago.'

Chigorin recoils. 'That's tough, Hootie. Ten days? You're not even adjusted yet.' He stands up and limps to the door. 'There's somethin' I have to do right now, but I'll come back in a few minutes. Then we'll get down to business.'

The Russian doesn't doubt Hootie, but he checks anyway. He runs Judson Hootier's rap sheet, noting the middle name, Two-Bears. Then he heads for the bathroom, feeling good about the future. Hootie's honesty was a concession and it's rapidly becoming clear that he's still a kid. Chigorin enters a stall, takes another pull on the flask, empties his bladder and washes his hands, all the while contemplating a full-out attack on Hootie Hootier's well-being.

Chigorin re-enters the room bearing another gift, a glazed doughnut wrapped in a paper towel. He lays the doughnut and towel before Hootie. 'In case you're hungry.'

Hootie starts to say thanks, but stops himself. The cop's pulled a card from the inside pocket of his jacket and he's reading off Hootie's rights. That done, he produces a form and a pen.

'Sign here.' He unfolds the form and pushes it in Hootie's direction. Hootie reads the form, taking his time, but there's nothing in it about waiving his rights and he signs without protest.

Chigorin slides the form into his pocket. 'I got some bad news for you, kid. I just got off the phone with your probation officer. He says if I wanna violate you, I should go ahead.'

'Violate me for what?' Hootie's heart nearly stops in his chest. The fall has been too steep and too quick. Despite the room and the cops and the fucking doughnut, some part of his brain insists this can't be happening. 'I haven't committed a crime.'

'Carrying false identification is a crime by itself. Plus, you're not livin' at the address you gave to your probation officer and the cellphone in your pocket is probably stolen.' Chigorin hesitates, but Hootie doesn't dispute any of his claims. 'And the worst part, the absolutely most fucked-up part, is that you're implicated in a homicide investigation. Hootie, I want you to sit back and look at the situation from your parole officer's point of view. You're only out of jail ten days and already you're a pain in his ass.'

'You can't put a murder on me,' Hootie finally says.

'No? Tell me where you were at three thirty-five on Monday morning.'

'Asleep in my bed.'

The Russian's mouth curls in distaste. 'What bed? Where?'

'Right where I was supposed to be. In my mom's apartment.'

'You sure about that, Hootie? Because lyin' to me is not gonna help your case. Not unless your goal is a cot on Rikers Island. Bear in mind, you'll be sitting in jail for a month before you even get a probation hearing. And if you should lose the hearing, you'll have to serve the two years still left on your sentence. That means upstate, Hootie. That means prison.'

Hootie surprises himself. Now that the cards are on the table, now that the threat is real, his mind's becoming focused. The cop's talk of Rikers Island has transported him right back to Otis Bantum and the mindset that allowed him to survive. Hootie was first challenged shortly after his assignment to a dormitory. The battle that followed, a battle he could not afford to lose, was especially brutal. As a parting gesture, he'd slammed the sole of his shoe into his unconscious opponent's bent knee.

'I was asleep in my bed,' Hootie repeats.

'You're sayin' that if I produce surveillance tape from the a hundred and forty-fifth street subway station, your face won't be on it? That what you're tellin' me?'

The questions cheer Hootie. If the cops have a surveillance tape, they must know that he didn't fire the gun.

'Before you jump to any foolish conclusions,' the cop adds, as though reading his mind, 'the tape in question shows the subway entrance, not the platform. So I know you jumped the turnstile and I know you

188

didn't run off when the shots were fired. What I don't know, and what you're gonna tell me, is what happened in between.'

When Hootie lets his hands fall into his lap, the keys Bubba dropped into his pocket jingle softly. Despite himself, he smiles.

Chigorin notes the smile, but says nothing. He's bluffing here. The shooting on Hamilton Place was called in at 3:25, exactly when, according to the surveillance tape, Hootie entered the subway station. He could not have killed Almeda.

'When I spoke to your parole officer, he told me that your middle name was Two-Bears. Is that right?'

Hootie hesitates before replying. Don't talk to cops was the common wisdom among his peers at the Otis Bantum Correctional Facility. Cops lie all the time and their promises are less sincere than the encouragement of street whores.

'Hey, I asked you a question,' the cops says.

Hootie leans forward before answering with a question of his own: 'Do you think I need a lawyer?'

'Only if you want me to violate you right now. Only if you want to be printed, photographed and strip-searched. Only if you want to spend the next two years in prison.'

'How does sending me to jail help you?'

'If you understood how cops think, you wouldn't be asking that question.' Very carefully, Chigorin crosses his legs. The pain at the back of his head is more or less constant now.

'And how do cops think?'

'Cops think taking a mutt like you off the street by any means available is a major victory. That's why I won't hesitate when it's time for me to testify. I'm gonna take the stand, swear to tell the truth, then claim that you're a vital witness in a homicide investigation. I'm gonna say that you're a vital witness, but you not only won't co-operate, you're a likely co-conspirator. See, I can put you in the station when the shots were fired, not only beyond a reasonable doubt, but beyond any doubt at all.'

Hootie runs his fingers through his short hair. He's thinking there's no jury at a probation hearing, only a judge who can pretty much do anything he wants. And the truth is that he was on the platform. He did see what happened and the best lawyer in New York won't be able to explain away his failure to cooperate. Which is not to say that he'll have the best lawyer in New York. Far from it.

Suddenly, the cops rises. 'Tell you what, Hootie, I'm gonna take a little break here, give you a chance to think it over while I talk to your partner. Who knows? Maybe he'll put the gun in your hand. Myself, I don't make you for a killer. But any port in a storm, right?'

FIFTEEN

Hootie's tempted to relax when the door shuts, but then he remembers the trick mirror on the wall. The cop might be watching – hell, a dozen cops might be watching – and he doesn't want to squirm. So, he stays right where he is, in his chair, and goes to work on the doughnut lying in front of him. The cop was right about making a choice, but not about the factors involved. Somebody, he or Bubba, has to get out tonight. Otherwise, Amelia ... But Hootie doesn't want to go there. He doesn't want to be distracted and he forces himself to answer what he now understands to be the only relevant question.

Will the cops release Bubba if Hootie Hootier refuses to cooperate?

Because if only one of them is free to help Amelia, Bubba's the logical choice. That bit about killing Sherman Cole's wife and kids?

Bubba's already killed two people, the first with his bare hands and the second in the coldest of cold blood. When the time comes, he won't hesitate.

But what if Hootie refuses to cooperate and Bubba's arrested anyway? What if they're both arrested? Bubba's on parole, not probation. He can be violated for any reason by any cop in the city. That means weeks on Rikers Island before he gets a hearing.

Initially, Hootie's unable to draw the logical conclusion. There's too much guilt in the way, too much street macho about not being a rat. At Otis Bantum, snitches were not tolerated. Even a rumor could get you shanked.

But it comes to him, finally. The only way to guarantee that somebody's out there to find Amelia is for Judson Two-Bears Hootier to put that gun in Bubba Yablonsky's hand. Otherwise, it's a toss of the dice.

Hootie draws this conclusion five minutes after the cop leaves. Then he gets to think about it, to stare at the closed door, to fight off a sense of relief that leaves him giddy.

Noble Hootie. Hootie the White Knight ... well, not exactly white, but what the fuck.

He can be the Beige Knight, or maybe the Mixed-Race Knight. According to Bubba, there's a gun in the apartment. The gun will be his lance, the Crown Vic his gallant steed. Hootie took a few drivers' ed classes before he dropped out of school. With luck, he might even get off the block without wrecking the car.

The Russian stops in the john for a quick drink, then heads for Bubba's room. He finds the man pretty much as he left him, a giant tethered to the Earth, his size now as much a liability as an asset. If he was less threatening, he wouldn't be handcuffed and shackled.

'Bad news for you, Bubba. Your pal ratted you out.' Chigorin drops on to the chair. He's expecting a heated reaction, but Yablonsky seems almost relieved. Instantly, the Russian's antennae begin to twitch. 'I mean, you can't blame the kid. Nineteen years old? Ten days out of jail? What would you do in his place?'

'Tell you to go fuck yourself, which I'm officially doing right now.'

Chigorin ignores the remark. 'Look, Bubba, if you have something to say, you'd best get it off your chest. I've got a surveillance tape that puts you on that platform and a witness who puts the gun in your hand. You hear what I'm sayin'? And there's somethin' else, too, somethin' you might not even know about. When you recovered those shell casings on the subway platform, you missed one. That's right. You missed a casing which we subsequently matched to the casings found next to Flaco Alameda's body. They were fired from the same gun. Your gun. Tell me something, Bubba, what the fuck were you thinkin' when you shot that rat? Was that some kind of psychotic breakdown?'

The last two questions produce the first discernible reaction in Bubba other than anger. His face reddens and he bites at his lower lip. 'Are you good at anything?' he asks.

'How good?'

'Better than almost anyone else on the planet.'

Chigorin thinks it over, then responds honestly: 'No.'

'So, you're just another cog in old wheel, mediocre, a nonentity.'

'I'm like everyone else. I'm the center of my own world.'

'That's good.' Bubba shifts in his seat, the chains that bind him clinking softly. 'But me, I was at the center of other people's worlds, or as close as another person can get. Every game I played, there were pro scouts in the stands. I got dozens of calls from agents who wanted a heads-up in case I decided to skip my senior year. And the money? All those zeroes? I could have lived forever on the money they were talkin' about.'

'I hear ya, Bubba, and I'm sympathetic. But some things you can't walk away from, like killin' a teammate.'

'It was a fight, nothin' more, a fight I didn't start. But the information the cops and the prosecutor leaked made it sound like I stalked the guy, like he was a helpless victim. Like he wasn't six-four and didn't weigh two hundred and twenty pounds and wasn't a trained athlete.' Bubba pauses long enough to shake his head in disgust. 'The worst part came at a press conference. Some reporter asked the prosecutor if the state was gonna charge me under the hate crimes statute. They weren't, of course, and the scumbag knew it. But what did he say? "We're not ruling anything out." Nice, right? By the time the case was ready to go to trial, the atmosphere was poisoned. That's the word my lawyer used: poisoned. If we put the case before a jury, he'd have two burdens. First, he'd have to prove me innocent beyond a reasonable doubt, then he'd have to overcome the charge that I was a racist.'

And that's all Bubba has to say. Chigorin's attempts to revive the conversation fail utterly and fifteen minutes later he walks out the door. The squad room is humming now as the detectives approach the end of their tour. Handcuffed to a bench, three perps talk loudly amongst themselves. They speak in rapid-fire Spanish, too fast for Chigorin to pick up more than a word or two. But he can hear the defiance in their tone. Macho, macho, macho. The Russian wonders who'll be the first to break, the flip from badass to cooperating witness being a phenomenon he's witnessed many times.

'Hey, Detective.'

Chigorin looks up to find Sergeant Vincenzo standing to his left. 'Sarge?'

'I gotta have one of the rooms.' Vincenzo strokes a silky mustache and smiles. He gestures to the men on the bench.

'No problem. The big one's on parole and I'm gonna violate him. You want, you can dump him in a cell till I get to the paper-work. Thing is, though, I could use a heads-up on the timing.'

Ten minutes later, Chigorin invades Hootie's little space. Right away, he knows something's hinky. The kid's looking directly into his eyes and he seems to have aged ten years.

'Up ya go,' Chigorin says, 'time to hit the john.'

The demand takes Hootie by surprise, but he recovers quickly. He walks past Chigorin and out the door just as two cops lead Bubba, still cuffed and shackled, across the squad room. Hootie turns, drawn by the sound of Bubba's rattling chains, and they look into each other's eyes for just a mo-ment. The Russian notes the pregnant nature of the exchange. These are two men in basic agreement.

Chigorin waits patiently by the door as Hootie goes about his business. He's in-trigued now, but exhausted as well. So tired, in fact, that he's thinking he'd better call his boss and ask for reinforcements, maybe Nick Campo. It's Nick's case, after all. But the Russian has a lot of cowboy in him and he decides to take one more shot at Hootie Hootier.

Good thing, too, because Hootie doesn't wait for Chigorin to open the conversation. The moment they're seated, he utters the magic words: 'What's in it for me?'

'Pardon?'

'I know what you want me to give you. What I don't know is what I get in return.'

The Russian smiles. 'You go to Catholic school when you were a kid?' he asks.

'What's it to you?' In fact, Hootie was educated in Catholic schools from kindergarten until the day he dropped out.

'I'm just thinkin', the way you talk, it's not street. So I was guessin' the nuns got their hands on you at some point in your life.'

Not only the nuns, but his mother, too. Corlie Hootier, now Corlie Couch, did not tolerate Ebonics in her home. On the other hand, her husband's Jamaican English was just fine, though it bore no resemblance to the grammar taught by the nuns at St. Catherine's.

'OK, forget it.' Chigorin's waves off his remark. 'I didn't mean anything special. I was just curious.'

Hootie finds himself disliking everything about the cop on the other side of the table: the overhanging forehead, like the brow of helmet, and the squinty little eyes, blue, naturally. The cop's short nose is pitted, his thin lips the color of gristle trimmed from a steak. His head is almost square, a block of stone with a bandage plastered to the back.

'You beat me down pretty good,' Hootie says. 'Now you gotta show some bling. What's in it for me?'

Chigorin nods in agreement. 'I know what you want, Hootie. You want to go home tonight. Well, I can arrange that, no problem. In fact, to be completely honest, I lied about calling your probation officer, so this whole business is just between the two of us.'

'That's great, but how do I know you're not lyin' now?'

The Russian raises a defensive hand. 'First, let me say that you have it exactly right. Cops do lie at the drop of a hat. We're supposed to. But you have a pair of hole cards, Hootie, and they're both wild. The most important is that any statement you give me tonight is so much toilet paper if you don't testify before the grand jury.'

'And the other one?'

'Like you said when I first came in, what crime have you committed? Carrying false ID? Hootie, we're talkin' about a murder. Now I know you don't think too much of cops in general, but this you can take to the bank. When it comes to cold-blooded executions, we care.'

The time has come and Hootie knows it. He looks to the mirror, then to the door, finally to Chigorin, whose expression hasn't changed.

'Alright, this is how it went down.'

Once started, Hootie relates a simple narrative. He begins his story in his mother's house, with his banishment. From there, with no money and no place to go, he walked directly to the subway and jumped the turnstile. Maybe five minutes later, Bubba Yablonsky, a complete stranger, took a seat next to him on the bench. They struck up a casual conversation, two dudes on the move in the wee hours of the morning, no big deal.

Enter the rat.

'I don't know what set him off. I made a little joke – when I noticed the rat, I said, "Dinner" – and the guy started blasting away.'

'And then what, you became friends? Shooting the rat was a bonding experience?'

'I was on the street with nowhere to go. You ever been on the street, Detective?'

'Can't say as I have.'

'Well, Bubba offered me a bed and I took it. Like you said, any port in a storm.'

'OK, I can see that. Only Bubba doesn't strike me as an altruistic kinda guy. So, what did he want from you?'

Hootie shakes his head. He's not going there. 'I'm puttin' the gun in Bubba's hand. I don't know what he did with it before he came into the subway. As for afterwards, all I can say is Bubba's a nice guy, a real saint. He sheltered me out of the goodness of his heart.'

Chigorin makes a little circling gesture with his forefinger. He's thinking now that the kid's too smart for his own good, that he needs to be put in his place. But there's still the million dollar question to be asked. 'So, what happened to the gun? Where is it now?'

'Bubba tossed it into the East River that same night.'

The Russian's heart sinks. He was hoping

the gun was still in the apartment. Recovering the murder weapon would seal the deal for Bubba Yablonsky.

'Where in the East River?'

'Between Fourteenth and Twenty-Third streets. We were walkin' along, just bullshitting, when he takes out the gun and says, "From the half-court line." Then he threw it about fifty feet into the water.'

Hootie's lying about where Bubba disposed of the gun. He's off by almost a half-mile and the Russian observes a very slight hesitation.

'Don't play with me, Hootie. Because if that gun turns up, I'll kick your ass from here to the Bronx.'

'The gun's in the water,' Hootie insists.

'You sure?'

'C'mon, man.'

Chigorin leans across the table. No more sweet talk. 'My name is Detective Chigorin, not man or bro or any other bullshit, and I'd strongly advise you not to disrespect me.' The Russian pauses, but Hootie seems neither afraid nor defiant. He seems preoccupied. 'Now you're gonna write out a statement and sign it. After that, you're going home to the address you gave your probation officer. And you're not gonna change your residence without calling me first. In fact, you're gonna call me every day no matter where you are. If ya don't, if you make me have to look for you, I'm gonna put a serious hurtin' on your ass. I'm not jokin' here.'

For the first time, the Russian's words produce a reaction. Hootie looks down at the table and he closes his eyes for a moment.

'Give me a break ... Detective. I didn't leave because I wanted to. My mother kicked me out.'

'Well, you're just gonna have to call her and make nice. I don't want you on the street and Bubba's apartment is off-limits until I get a search warrant. Make no mistake, Hootie. This is a murder investigation. If you get in the way, you'll think you fell under the wheels of a city bus.'

Now that he's repeated the basic message for the third time, Chigorin eases up. He furnishes Hootie with pen, paper and his personal cellphone, then leaves the room to call his boss, Lieutenant Hamilton. He knows the job will never agree to fund a scuba team. Almeda doesn't rate that kind of attention. Plus, the East River is actually a tidal basin with the tides commonly running better than six knots. By now, the weapon could be a mile away, or buried under a foot of silt. But the Russian tries anyway. Without the weapon to confirm Hootie's statement, the case against Bubba is very thin.

Generally affable, Lieutenant Hamilton listens without interruption as Chigorin explains the situation, beginning with the unexpected call from his snitch. Then he echoes the Russian's doubts.

'If the weapon's really in the river, forget about a recovery operation. And as for Yablonsky, he's not goin' anywhere, so there's no reason to make an arrest tonight. Try to find that homeless guy instead. What'd you say he was?'

'Hunch-backed.'

'Yeah, find him, see if he can pick Yablonsky out of a line-up.'

Chigorin stifles a laugh, imagining a line-up that includes six normal-sized human beings and Bubba Yablonsky. Talk about a fix. But the other alternative, convincing six Bubba-sized volunteers to appear in a line-up, is clearly impossible.

'I think I'm gonna pass,' he tells his boss. 'I'll do the paperwork on Yablonsky and get the kid's statement. From there, it's up to Campo. I'm not feelin' all that good. I gotta get some sleep.'

'No problem. If Campo has any questions, he'll give you a call. And by the way, you did great work here. I didn't think we had a chance in hell of clearing the Almeda shooting and now we got ourselves a genuine celebrity. Congratulations.'

Hootie stares down at Chigorin's cellphone. He's pissed off even thinking about Archie Couch. But the cop's not bluffing. Hootie's either going back to his mother's apartment or back to Rikers Island.

The choice is pretty simple, but Hootie doesn't pick up Chigorin's phone, not right away. Instead his thoughts drift to the vision Bubba described – Bubba and Amelia both. How many times did Eli Scannon warn him against being seduced by the white man's fantasies? And what exactly does he owe Amelia? On the one hand, his every instinct is to ride to her rescue. But there's this little voice now, whispering into his ear, gentle as a breeze. From the drug dealer's murder to the sale of the Cookinarts, each link in the chain was forged before Hootie joined the team. So why is he now responsible for the consequences? Why should he risk his freedom for Amelia Cincone?

Hootie picks up the phone without answering the question. He dials his home number and his mother picks up on the second ring.

'Hootie, I've been so worried,' she tells him. 'Why haven't you called me?'

SIXTEEN

The night ends for Hootie in a series of embarrassments. First thing, the cop baby-sits him all the way to the front door of his building. There's another lecture, too, complete with threats, about staying in touch. And what can Hootie do except agree? Agree when he's imagining what it'd be like to drive his fist into the cop's lipless mouth.

As he gets out of the car, Hootie wonders if he's supposed to say thank you. Thank you for not throwing me in jail. Thank you for making me a snitch. Thank you for putting me on a collision course with the wrath of Corlie Couch.

Only it's not wrath that Hootie faces when he walks into his mother's home at one o'clock in the morning. No, Corlie's round face and large green eyes display equal measures of grief and disappointment. Her son has failed her again. Her boy child, her little man.

Hootie's not a parent and he has only a vague notion of how parents relate to their children. Nevertheless, just for a moment he quite literally feels her pain. Call it empathy, but her dashed hopes for her boy reach in to grip his heart. All that promise washed into the storm drains along with the rest of the trash. Headed for the ultimate sewage treatment plant, the one called prison.

A memory flashes through Hootie's mind, a young boy flying into his mother's arms. After Hootie's father died, Corlie supported her family by working seventy-hour weeks. Though he was too young to realize it, when she finally did come home, usually hauling bags of groceries, she must have been teetering on the brink of exhaustion. But she didn't refuse him the comfort of her arms. Never, not once. Always, she laid the grocery bags on the floor, dropped to her knees and spread her arms wide.

'Come to me, boy child.'

So what can Hootie say now? What can he do except repeat the same lie he told her over the phone? The cops are hassling him simply because he's a black man living on the street. If she refuses him a place to stay, he's certain to be violated, since the terms of his probation require him to have a fixed address. Plus, without that fixed address, gainful employment is out of the question.

For once, Corlie Couch doesn't have much to say. Maybe she's resigned, maybe she's already mourning his loss. Or maybe she's consoling herself. Her daughter's an attorney. One out of two ain't bad.

Either way, she disappears into the bedroom ten minutes after Hootie's arrival, leaving him to sit all by his lonesome in her crowded living room. Back in the day, Corlie's furnishings were purchased, one piece at a time, from crappo furniture stores on Third Avenue, stores that specialized in low-end merchandise and high-interest credit. No more. Corlie's pearl-gray sofa sweeps across two walls. Along with her glass coffee table, the ceramic lamps on the end tables and the carpet beneath his feet, the sofa was purchased from Thomasville, and not at a clearance sale, either.

Respectability. Sometimes Hootie believes that respectability is all his mother's ever wanted. Corlie's parents were migrants from rural Mississippi, educated at Jim Crow schools and raised on farms where they were put to work almost as soon as they could walk. Their skills were particularly unsuited to New York with its eroded manufacturing base, and though both worked, every month began with a struggle to pay the bills. Which ones had to be paid, which could be put off. Hootie knows all this because his mother's economic struggles were a preoccupation in the Hootier household. Rip his pants in the school yard? Stains on his new winter coat? Sometimes the lecture went on for days.

That all changed on the day his mother married Archie Couch. Corlie's respectable now, her life tidy and ordered. With a single exception, of course.

Hootie's mind is swirling, with thoughts and emotions. His mother's home is one big reproach. And then there's Amelia. And Bubba in a cell. And that fucking cop. Hootie doesn't doubt, not for a minute, that Chigorin will make good on his threats if he doesn't cooperate.

It's two o'clock when Hootie lays his head on the pillow. He's thinking that sleep is a real long-shot, but he drops off within seconds. When he awakens, it's nine thirty and the apartment's empty, his mother and stepfather having gone off to work. He jerks upright, coming out of bed as though in response to a fire. Sixteen hours. That's how long Amelia's been gone.

Now Hootie's faced with another decision, courtesy of Bubba Yablonsky who stuck those keys in his pocket. And he's not unmindful of the fact that his first decision, to throw in with Bubba, didn't exactly work out. No, that particular fact occupies the exact center of his consciousness, solid as a tumor.

Hootie trots off to the bathroom. He uses the toilet, showers and shaves, finally dresses. Now what? A bowl of cereal? He looks out through the front windows at a bright blue sky – after weeks of brown summer haze, the intensity is almost surreal. Hootie's thinking that what he really ought to do is take a long walk in Riverside Park, maybe up to the George Washington Bridge where he knows a player who sells top-of-the-line powder. He can hang there, too, maybe come home after his mother and Archie go to bed, start again tomorrow morning. He's got a phone number as well, a number given to him in Otis Bantum by a professional burglar named Reef who specializes in commercial burglaries. That's because commercial break-ins aren't considered violent crimes and New York's three-strikes law, with its draconian sentences, doesn't apply.

Hootie's sitting on the edge of the bed, lost in thought, when the phone rings. He crosses to the living room and checks the caller ID screen. His mother's cellphone number. Hootie's not really tempted to answer, but he continues to stare down for a moment. Then he turns abruptly and leaves the apartment, pausing only to lock the door on his way out.

The streets are teeming, as always in the summer. Moms in lawn chairs, kids tearing down the sidewalk on tricycles, bicycles and skateboards. One of Hootie's neighbors, Buford Parks, sits in a wheelchair, attended by a home health aide. Buford lost both legs in Vietnam and he's been sitting in front of the building ever since.

'Yo, Hootie, that you, boy? Come close. I can't see for shit no more.'

'Yeah, it's me, Buford. What's up with you?'

'Same old same old.'

'I hear that. Where's Beatrice?'

'Beatrice gone six months now, Hootie. Stroke took her.'

'I'm sorry to hear that, man.'

'It's OK, Hootie. She's with the Lord now.'

Hootie taps Buford's shoulder, then passes on down the street, dodging the kids, to Broadway. He stands on the corner for a moment, then raises his arm to hail a gypsy cab. When a gray Lincoln pulls over, he gives the driver Bubba's address on the Lower East Side, then negotiates a price: $23.

Hootie's too preoccupied to enjoy the views across the East River on the trip downtown. He's just remembered that according to Bubba, Sherman Cole lives out in Queens, in a neighborhood called Bayside. Hootie has no idea where Bayside is. Somewhere beyond Flushing, the last stop on the 7 line, would be his guess, but that covers a lot of territory. Hootie's been to Hollis in Queens, to the home of his Auntie Grace. He remembers children riding bicycles on quiet streets, a trellis of red roses in the back yard, chickens lined up on a barbecue grill. All very nice, he has to admit, but so alien it might be another planet.

The driver pulls to a halt behind a bus at 10th Street and Hootie gets out. He heads for Bubba's Crown Vic, half hoping it won't start. That would narrow his options by a good deal. But when he twists the key in the ignition, the engine leaps into life.

Hootie shuts the car down and heads up to the apartment. It's becoming painfully obvious to Hootie that Bubba expected him to snitch, that he knew Hootie would cave when he dropped the keys into Hootie's pocket. Does that mean Bubba trusted Hootie to go to Amelia's rescue? Or that Hootie was her only hope?

Hootie pauses with his back against the door. His mind turns to Amelia for just a moment, to her present, assuming she still has a present. But he doesn't allow himself to become overwhelmed. He heads off to Bubba's room in search of a gun. Again, he's half hoping that Bubba was lying, or that the weapon Bubba spoke of is locked in a safe. He opens the drawers in the bureau and rummages through the underwear and socks and stacked shirts. Beneath a neatly folded turtleneck sweater, he discovers a roll of fifty-dollar bills which he pockets without thinking twice. He tries the nightstands next, but one drawer is empty, while the other contains only a book: *Starting an On-line Business.*

Bubba's closet comes next and it's here, on a shelf, that Hootie finds a snub-nosed .38 revolver in a nylon ankle holster. He takes the weapon down and lays it on the bed. In New York, the minimum mandatory sentence for illegal possession of a handgun is three and a half years, which is why Hootie's never carried one. So this is a big moment for a nineteen-year-old kid, a can't-take-it-back moment, and Hootie's well aware of it.

Again, he asks himself what he owes Amelia. He's thinking that Eli Scannon would laugh in his face if asked the same question.

'The black man does not ride to the white man's rescue. The black man does not slay the dragon. Uh-uh. The black man most likely is the dragon. The black man is the one on the wrong end of the lance.'

Hootie laughs softly. He can hear Eli's voice, the tone midway between outraged and dismissive, the pitch rising at the end of each sentence. 'Boy, you must be crazy.'

Leaving the gun on the bed, Hootie trots off to Amelia's bedroom with its shag rug and ruffled bedspread. He boots up her computer, only to find it password protected. In the movies, there's always some kid who can unlock a hard drive with a few keystrokes, but he's not that kid. He shuts the computer down and begins to rummage through Amelia's drawers. Hootie's in search of more information on Sherman Cole, his address at the very least. He does not have far to look. The first drawer he opens, in the nightstand to the right of the bed, contains a photo of a house with an address on the back, as well as a bound Hagstrom *5 Borough Atlas.* The atlas is conveniently open to page ten and a block is circled. Hootie leans in close to read the small print: 27th Avenue off 215th Street.

A weapon, a car and a place to start. Strike one, strike two, strike three.

Hootie walks into the kitchen. He opens the refrigerator, discovers a container of orange juice and pours himself a glass. But he can't bring himself to drink. He lays the glass on the counter and heads back to Bubba's bedroom. Hootie's thinking he can at least go out there, to Bayside, and look around. But the idea makes him very uneasy. The house in the photo is a sprawling, three-story Tudor with an expanse of manicured lawn in front. That it belongs to a rich white man living in a rich white neighborhood is painfully obvious.

Hootie turns to catch his reflection in a full-length mirror on the back of a closet door. He tells himself he's not subject to the law against driving while black. Then he tells himself again. He understands, for the first time, exactly what Bubba meant when he said, 'You could be anyone.'

And Hootie understands, as well, that nothing Eli Scannon told him applies to his own life. Hootie's only the besieged black man in one of Scannon's many lectures if he chooses to be. Which is not to say Hootie discounts Scannon's wisdom. Hootie's been stopped by cops too many times, as have all his friends. White cops, black cops and Latino cops.

'Put ya fuckin' hands on the wall.'

If you mess with them, give them any lip, they'll put you on your face on the sidewalk, drop a knee across the back of your neck, cuff your hands behind your back, pepper spray you, slam a fist into your ribs. There's no telling in advance how far they'll go, a fact his mother stated clearly in a talk she gave him on his tenth birthday, a talk that boiled down to a simple maxim: don't fuck with cops.

Hootie picks up the holster and straps it to his right ankle, snugging the Velcro straps into place. He stands up and examines himself in the mirror. The legs of the chinos Bubba laid on him are wide enough to fully conceal the .38. He could be anybody. But Hootie's not anybody. He's Judson Two-Bears Hootier, a fact of life that becomes only too apparent when a pounding on the door is followed by the voice of Peter Chigorin.

'Answer the door, Hootie. And don't even consider about goin' rabbit on me. The knucklehead cop I got stationed outside has strict instructions to break your arm if you come down that fire escape.'

SEVENTEEN

The Russian hesitates before knocking on the door. He's been sitting in his car for the past twenty minutes, wondering how to play Hootie Hootier. The kid's defied him, no question about that. Chigorin specifically ordered Hootie to stay away from the apartment, not once but several times. What's more, he added a consequence, an ass-kicking which he'd ordinarily deliver without hesitation. Never mind the limp and the headache that won't go away no matter how many aspirins he takes. A promise is a promise.

But Chigorin's curious by nature, like most detectives. There's something's going down here and he wants to know what it is. Hootie didn't make an appearance this morning because he discounted Chigorin's threats. Hootie's too smart for that. So, if he came back anyway, he has to have a good reason.

The Russian's hoping it's money, a big fat wad of untraceable cash. That would solve a lot of problems. Already this morning he's fielded two calls from Yolanda. Was he gonna come up with the money for Sonia's camp or was he gonna crap out, just like he crapped out on their marriage?

But even if there's not a penny in the whole apartment, there's still the missing weapon. It's entirely possible that disposing of the gun is Hootie's sole aim, that he lied when he told Chigorin that Bubba threw it into the river. Recovering the murder weapon would solve almost as many problems as finding the money.

'C'mon, Hootie, I know you're in there.'

A door opens behind Chigorin, a neighbor. He flashes his shield without turning around. A moment later, the door in front of him swings open to reveal Hootie. Hootie's standing with his feet apart, shoulders spread, but the Russian shoves him out of the way and walks into the apartment.

Though Chigorin's not crazy about modern furniture, he has to admit that he's impressed. The furniture, the drapes, the lamps and tables and the rug, they come off as elements of a single, ultra-clean design. Color and shape, everything fits, including the abstract paintings on the walls. The place has the feel of an expensive hotel room.

'Close the door,' he calls over his shoulder.

Hootie looks down the hallway. It's maybe twenty feet to the staircase and the cop's sporting a limp. No way could Hootie be caught, not unless there really is another cop waiting outside, which he doesn't believe. But he doesn't run, either. He closes the door and locks it.

When Hootie turns, the cop's already in the living room, sitting in one of two small armchairs facing the couch. He gestures to the other chair and says, 'What am I gonna do with you? Because I gotta say, your act is wearin' thin.'

Chigorin leans back in his chair and lets his eyes criss-cross Hootie's body, searching for a gun. But Hootie's polo shirt is tucked into his cotton slacks and there's no telltale bulge in his pockets. In fact, he looks more like a college freshman than a Rikers Island graduate. If he told you he was pre-med at Columbia, you'd buy the con without thinking twice. Nevertheless, he lacks experience and it's obvious. The tension's apparent in his eyes and in his hands, which are curled almost into fists, and in the way he shifts his weight from one foot to the other. The kid wants Chigorin gone, but he's not helping himself by advertising the fact.

The Russian's out of uniform, no brown suit today. He's wearing a linen sports jacket over a pair of jeans and a sea-blue shirt. A leather briefcase hangs from a strap on his right shoulder. There's only one item in the briefcase, a pint of vodka. Chigorin retrieves the bottle and takes a quick swig.

'You like stories, Hootie?' he asks.

Hootie forces himself not to recoil. He's thinking that getting hassled by cops is a birthright – nothing personal, ha-ha. But what did he do to deserve this psycho drunk? What god did he offend? Still, Hootie has a point to make and he refuses to be deflected.

'Lemme lay this out for you, Detective...'

'Chigorin.'

'Detective Chigorin, you got no cause to hound me. I wrote out a statement last night and put my name to it. Plus, I'm ready to testify whenever you want. To me, that sounds like cooperation, but here you are, all up in my face when I'm just goin' about my business.'

'See, right there, Hootie, that's not right. I told you not to come back to this apartment.' The Russian's tone is almost pleading. As though he wants to be understood. 'And I thought I made myself very clear. Or at least I tried to.'

'But that's the whole point. This apartment's not a crime scene and I didn't break in. I have the keys. So, what right do you have to tell me where I can't go?'

With some difficulty, the Russian stands up. His ankle is hurting him worse than ever and there's pus in the wound. He saw it this morning when he put on his socks.

'Actually,' he admits, with a quick grin, 'your bein here is a lucky break for me. I had no way to get inside without ya. Now I'm gonna toss the apartment and I want you to stay close while I'm doin' it. *Comprende?*'

The Russian's search is thorough, but he finds neither gun nor money, only an ounce or so of marijuana which he leaves in a drawer. Still, the effort bears fruit. There's a female currently in residence, a girl by the look of the clothing in her closet. Another piece of the puzzle.

The search takes over an hour, with Hootie becoming more and more impatient as the minutes pass. By the time Chigorin limps back to his chair and sits down again, Hootie's fingers are trembling.

'You satisfied now?' he asks.

Chigorin points to the chair next to his. 'So, what I asked you before. Do ya like stories? I mean, when they're told well?'

'Man, I don't have time for this bullshit.'

'There's where you're wrong, Hootie. You're here until I let you go. And make no mistake about it. I could have you held as a material witness right this minute. See, that's where you made your mistake, when you wrote out that statement. Because I'm tellin' ya, there's not a judge in this city who won't lock your ass up if I claim you're a flight risk. But that's not where I'm goin', Hootie. I'm not here to play macho cop.'

Suddenly, Hootie feels the weight of the revolver strapped to his ankle. Three and a half years minimum, mandatory. He watches Chigorin take another hit on the vodka. 'There's no cop downstairs,' he says.

'Yeah, that's true. I lied about that.' Chigorin puts the bottle away. He folds his hands in his lap and raises his head to meet Hootie's gaze. 'There's a guy I know, Eugene Blau, had a life like you wouldn't believe. He does three tours in 'Nam, from Sixty-Nine right to the end, Special Forces all the way. After that, he emigrates to Israel where he goes to work for the Mossad – he's already in Beirut, stirring up trouble between the Christians and the Arabs when Israel invades Lebanon in Eighty-Two. A year later he's kidnapped by Syrian secret police. They hold him in Southern Lebanon for ten months – under brutal conditions, of course – until he's finally rescued. Hootie, Eugene's Arabic is perfect and you can bet the Mossad does everything it can to make him stay on. But Eugene finds religion in prison. He's a changed man. In Nineteen Eighty-Six, he returns to the USA and joins a Hasidic sect, the Lubavitchers in Crown Heights. For the next ten years, he studies the Torah and the Talmud, along with all the commentaries, syllable by syllable. But he doesn't find God. No, what happens is that he becomes a total drunk, which is how we finally met.'

Hootie drops into the chair. The cop has worn him down. 'You're fuckin' crazy,' he says, as much to himself as to Chigorin. 'There's no point to what you're sayin'.'

'Stories, Hootie, that's the point. Eugene told stories like nobody else. Amazing stories. When he was broke, I used to buy him drinks just to hear him.' Chigorin crosses his legs and begins to probe his ankle. 'Turn out your pockets,' he says.

'What?'

'Turn out your pockets.'

'Man, I'm not—'

'Turn out your pockets or I'll cuff your hands and turn 'em out myself.'

Hootie's so mad he can barely speak, but he complies, nevertheless. He places the items he retrieves, including the roll of fifties, on the table between them. Chigorin picks up the roll and counts it. He's thinking that Hootie will cave within the next fifteen minutes, thirty at most. Whatever's eating him, it's stuck in his throat. If he doesn't cough it up, he'll choke.

'So, tell me about the girl who lives here.' Chigorin waves off the request before Hootie can reply. 'Oh, wait, there's somethin' I wanna tell ya first. Before I forget, which I have a habit of doing these days. It's about your pal, Bubba. See, shooting Flaco, this I can understand, money being money. But the rat doesn't make any sense. Hear what I'm sayin'? If it wasn't for the rat, I wouldn't have shit in the way of physical evidence. So, why'd he do that?'

Hootie shrugs, the gesture mechanical. Amelia's fate is resting on his shoulders, heavy as lead, and the seconds are ticking by, each one a nail in her coffin. Despite the cop's drunken bullshit, one thing's perfectly clear. Whoever snatched Amelia can't let her go.

'Anyway,' Chigorin continues, 'I made a call to the Department of Corrections while I waited for you to show up. Seems like your pal, Bubba Yablonsky, was an asshole of the first magnitude. Now there's a lot of gambling in prison, which I'm sure you already know, and Bubba was right in the middle of it. He was smuggling dope, too. We're talkin' about a guy who was transferred eleven times in ten years, but who got in trouble everywhere he went. He was in a dozen fights and he's suspected of beating a prison guard half to death.'

'What does that mean? Suspected?'

'Good question, Hootie – one that occurred to me, too. So I called the Menands

Correctional Facility and spoke to a deputy warden named Granger. According to the victim of the assault, he was hit from behind and lost consciousness immediately. He never saw his attacker. Meantime, every snitch in the institution pointed a finger at Bubba Yablonsky.'

Hootie starts to say something, then stops as a question jumps into his mind. What would happen if he laid the whole story on Detective Chigorin? If he admitted to every element, including the blackmail? If he laid the burden on someone else's shoulders?

'Granger knew Bubba well, Hootie,' the Russian continues. 'Bubba worked in his office for a time. He says that Bubba has a great rap. You're with him for ten minutes, he's your new best pal. But there's a dark side, too, a wildness that Bubba can't tame. There was a murder in the prison, right before the guard was attacked. Bubba couldn't have committed the murder because he was playing basketball in front of two hundred or so fans, including the warden. But his hands were all over it.'

Chigorin pauses for breath. He's got the kid's full attention now. 'So, tell me about the girl who lives here. What's her name?'

'It's not your business.'

'Wrong, Hootie. Bubba's a murderer. His business, including anyone he's living with, is my business. I'm surprised you can't see that.'

'Well, nothin' says I have to help you.'

'See, there you go again. Gettin' all defiant when I'm the one holding the club. But I don't wanna go there, like I already said. No, what I wanna do is hear the story. The whole story, from beginning to end. And I'm prepared to wait until hell freezes over.'

Chigorin underlines his point by taking another drink. He offers the bottle to Hootie, but Hootie merely shakes his head. Finally, he stuffs it into his briefcase and relaxes. Outside, a jackhammer begins to pound, the din a counterpoint to the seconds passing by. Hootie manages to control himself for several minutes, merely crossing and uncrossing his legs. But the tension is finally too much for him. He stands up, walks to the window and stares down at the street through the branches of raggedy ginkgo. On the corner, a single Con Edison worker leans forward to place his full weight on the jackhammer. The man wears a blue hard hat with an American flag decal over the brim. A few feet away, six co-workers observe his progress.

'Why do cops have to be scumbags?' Hootie asks.

'Gimme a break. If you had to spend your working life around rapists and murderers, you'd be a scumbag, too. I mean, it's not like you're cooperating.'

'What if I can't cooperate? What then?'

Chigorin suppresses a grin. 'Like, if telling me the truth implicates you in a crime?'

'Yeah, like that.'

'Is it a worse crime than murder?'

Suddenly, Hootie begins to laugh. The way Bubba told it, the most beautiful part of the scam was that Cole, being a pedophile, couldn't go to the cops. Now Hootie's in exactly the same position. The joke's on him. He closes his eyes for a moment, trying to focus, but his adrenals are still pumping away, his thoughts zipping through his brain like fragments from a soft-nosed .22.

'No,' he finally says.

'How 'bout rape?'

'No.'

'Is it a violent crime of any type?'

That stops Hootie long enough to latch on

to a thought. Violent? Maybe he should ask Amelia before he answers the question. He turns away from the window and his eyes sweep across the room, the furniture and the artwork, that good-old cracker bling. All part of the seduction, of course, Bubba's seduction, with Hootie playing the unspoiled virgin.

'You once asked me what I was,' Hootie says. 'Well, my mother is black and my father was a Crow Indian. What do ya think that makes me?'

Chigorin hesitates for a moment, then observes, 'If your mother was white, you'd be a half-breed. I don't know what happens if your mother's black. But I'll tell ya this, Hootie, the way you look, you can be anyone you wanna be.'

'That's what Bubba said.' Hootie lets it go for a few beats, but the cop doesn't respond. Finally, he says, 'Amelia. The girl who lives here, her name is Amelia.'

'And where is she now?'

'That's a long story.'

'Hootie, I'm all ears.'

EIGHTEEN

It's a good story. No, a great story. Kallmann syndrome, pedophiles in the park, surveillance cameras built into clocks and air purifiers, online seduction, extortion, kidnapping. And what about those defective Cookinarts, a sample of which Hootie produces?

'The guy dreams big,' Chigorin finally admits, his tone admiring. 'I'm talkin' about Bubba. He thinks long-term.'

'Bubba and Amelia, both. Amelia's nineteen going on a hundred.'

'And you? What was your take on the scam?'

'The way they laid it out, I figured we couldn't fail.'

The Russian gets to his feet. He's thinking that he'll have to see a doctor before long. His ankle is noticeably swollen and hot to the touch. But there's no backing off now that he knows what happened. And there's no time for a standard investigation, either. There's just him and the kid and the need to move fast.

'Tell me what Sherman Cole looks like.' Chigorin's already walking toward the door. 'How old was he?'

'In his late thirties.'

'Describe him.'

Hootie follows Chigorin into the hallway, pausing only to lock up before heading down the stairs. The Russian's just ahead, leaning hard on the banister as he descends. Though he's obviously hurting, he doesn't complain.

'Average height, under six feet, but built strong. Not thick like Bubba, more like a bodybuilder. His hair's dark – maybe too dark, like he dyes it – and he has a mustache. Other than that, he looked ordinary.'

'That's it? What color were his eyes?'

'I got no idea. I was a hundred feet away. But I'll know him if I see him.'

'That's why you're comin' with me out to Bayside. If a citizen's life is in immediate danger, I have the authority to conduct a search without gettin' a warrant. So, I need you to ID Sherman Cole.'

Chigorin opens the lobby door and steps out on to the sidewalk. After days of intense summer heat, the cool breeze feels somehow alien. He pauses for a moment, turning his face into the wind, then limps off toward his car. 'How did Bubba identify Sherman Cole?'

'From his cellphone number. At least, that's what Amelia told me.'

'See, that should have set off the alarm bells right there. You can block caller ID just by dialing star-six-seven.'

'He tried that, but Amelia forced him to unblock his number. Threatened to cut him loose if he didn't. Look, I only came in at the end, but I know Bubba and Amelia were months setting this up.' Hootie's feeling a lot better now that he's unburdened himself. He slides into the car on the passenger's side, mindful of the weapon strapped to his ankle. 'The thing about Cole was that he had the money to pay off. So you could say we got too greedy.'

'Don't be hard on yourself. Given the number of wild cards in the pedophile deck, there was always a chance that you'd turn up a sociopath.'

Hootie fastens his seat belt as Chigorin

pulls out of the parking space. Not a bad idea, as it happens. Their route takes them along a series of highways: FDR Drive across the Triborough Bridge to the Grand Central Parkway, to the Whitestone Expressway, to the Cross Island Parkway. The cop pushes the speed limit hard, weaving in and out of traffic, cutting in front of irate drivers, pulling on to the shoulder when an accident brings them to a halt by LaGuardia Airport. He doesn't slow down until they leave the parkway at Bell Boulevard. Then he pulls to the curb in front of a restaurant and slams the transmission into park.

'We're two minutes from the address on that map,' he announces, 'and we need to get squared away. But first, lemme ask you this. If I didn't show up this morning, what did you plan to do?'

Hootie's looking over Chigorin's shoulder at the arc of a long suspension bridge. He doesn't know the name of the bridge, or where it comes down on the other end. The Bronx, he guesses. Connecticut would be too far.

'I was gonna drive out here and find Sherman Cole.'

'And then what?'

'Kill his dog.'

'Say again?'

'That's what Bubba said he was gonna do. Kill his wife, kill his kids, kill his dog.'

Chigorin's laugh, as he reaches into his briefcase, is short and harsh. Hootie averts his eyes, looking past the cop and out over the choppy waters of ... of what? The East River? The Hudson? There are sailboats out on the water, and a little band of fishing boats anchored beneath the bridge. He watches a fisherman cast a metallic lure in a long arc, from the shadows into the sun-light.

'Look, Hootie, even if Cole is at the ad-dress, that doesn't mean we'll find Amelia. In fact, when you think about it, his home is the last place he'd bring her. And you can't assume that he really lives there. Cellphones are cloned every day.'

Hootie turns his head to stare out through the windshield at the road ahead. He's thinking, If Sherman Cole lives in that house, Hootie Hootier will find Amelia, dead or alive. And not tomorrow, either. That's because Bubba was right. Kill his wife, kill his kids, kill his fucking dog.

The cop's made Hootie's life a lot easier,

whether he knows it or not. Sherman Cole wasn't responsible for Hootie's indecision. Hootie's problem was functioning in a rich white neighborhood. Now he can let the cop function for him. He doesn't have to learn on the fly.

'So what I want you to do is keep your mouth shut,' Chigorin continues. 'If you spot Cole, stick your right hand into your pocket, but don't say anything. That OK with you?'

Hootie pretends to consider the question. Finally, he says, 'Hey, you're the expert.'

Only a few miles from Chigorin's home in College Point, Bayside is familiar ground to the Russian. He pilots his car past a large garden apartment complex, then an upscale shopping center, to 27th Avenue, where he makes a left turn on to a block of large single-family homes set on generous lots. The architecture, except for the occasional McMansion, is a mix of colonial, ranch and Tudor homes. Chigorin has come to hate the McMansions. The other houses are set well back from the road, with spacious lawns and elaborate gardens, while the Mc-Mansions, with their columns and turrets and faux balconies, crowd up close to the sidewalks like inner-city apartment buildings. Chigorin's heard that these enormous homes are owned almost exclusively by Asians. If so, they've jettisoned the Eastern concepts of grace and harmony.

But Sherman Cole's home on a cul-de-sac is not a McMansion. It's a three-story Tudor with fluted chimneys at either end of a slate roof. On the lower floor, the windows are multi-paned and leaded. Half-timbers crisscross the stucco façade, while dormer windows project from the attic. The grounds are immaculate, the lawn so green, even in midsummer, that it might have been ordered whole from a seed catalog.

Chigorin nods to himself. Money, money, money. In his experience, you can't intimidate wealthy people. To the wealthy, cops are little more than servants. Or better yet, security guards charged with safeguarding their persons and property.

'Remember what I said,' the Russian tells Hootie as he opens the door and eases his left foot on to the road. 'We're only here to make an ID. If Cole's in the house, I'm gonna call for backup before I force my way inside.'

239

Chigorin limps along a flagstone path to a pair of heavily-carved doors. The doors are windowless, but a security camera to his right corrects that defect. The security camera is bolted to the stucco wall ten feet above his head.

The Russian glances into the lens without changing expression, then rings the bell. A moment later, the door on his right swings out to reveal the ugliest man he's ever seen. Little more than a slash, the man's wide mouth curls downward to frame a jaw that might be used to scoop flour from a bin. His large eyes bulge from his head, round as golf balls, yet his pupils are no more than smudges behind lids drawn so close he might be peering between the slats of a Venetian blind.

'May I help you?' the man asks.

Chigorin notes the careful enunciation, each word distinct. He's reminded of the butlers in English movies, how their diction is always more precise than the aristocrats they serve. But the man doesn't have a British accent and he's not a servant. He's dressed in wool slacks and a cardigan sweater, and his leather slippers are worn shiny by use.

'Detective Chigorin,' the Russian announces, displaying his badge and his ID. 'I'm looking for Sherman Cole.'

When the man smiles, the corners of his mouth rise to form a perfect smiley-face. 'That would be me,' he says. 'Won't you come in?'

'Thanks.' Chigorin walks past Cole into an oak-paneled foyer, with Hootie following behind. The foyer is six-sided, with a yellow-brown stone floor. From the ceiling directly above Chigorin's head, a glass fixture in the shape of a tulip hangs from a delicate chain, fixing the detective in a circle of light.

Chigorin studies Cole for a moment, but he can't get past the man's looks. Cole's thick eyebrows poke up in every direction, while his receding forehead runs backward to merge with a nearly bald scalp. From the neck down, he appears to be in his forties. From the neck up, he might be sixty.

'Say, would it be alright if we sat down?' the Russian asks. 'I got bit by a dog yesterday and my ankle's killing me.'

'Certainly.'

Cole leads Chigorin and Hootie into the living room. Large enough to accept the

Russian's entire apartment, the room is filled to overflowing with Victorian furniture,
most of it mismatched and all showing signs
of wear. But Chigorin doesn't sense neglect.
It's more like Cole's preserving the family
heirlooms. Every object is free of dust, including a series of ornately-framed land-
scapes.

Chigorin takes a seat and Hootie joins
him. Cole remains standing. He extends a
hand and says, 'May I offer you some re-
freshment? Coffee? Tea? A soft drink, perhaps?'

'Maybe a soft drink, a Coke if you have
one.' The Russian turns to Hootie. 'How
'bout you?'

Hootie nods, the gesture a bit too vehe-
ment, and Chigorin represses a frown. But
Cole appears not to notice. He leaves the
room, seemingly in no hurry, returning a
few minutes later, tray in hand. The tray
holds two Cokes in small green bottles and
a pair of ice-filled tumblers garnished with
wedges of lemon. Cole puts the tray on a
leather hassock, then finds a seat of his own
in a brocaded wing chair.

Chigorin fills a glass, squeezes in a few
drops of lemon, finally drinks. He replaces

the glass on the tray and smiles at Sherman Cole. 'There's nothin' like a Coke when you're really thirsty. Talk about an endorphin rush. I think I just satisfied ten different needs simultaneously.'

The Russian's looking into Cole's eyes, or as much of them as he can see. But Cole's heavy lids don't so much as quiver. He crosses his legs at the knees and folds his hands in his lap, then says, 'I'm glad you enjoyed it. I don't get many guests since my wife passed on. I'm afraid my social skills need polishing.'

Chigorin drinks again. 'You're doin' just fine, Mr. Cole, and please let me apologize in advance for imposing myself.'

'Always glad to cooperate. Support your police and all that.'

'I only wish everybody thought like you. Where I work, cooperation is hard to come by. In fact, I'm more likely to be on the wrong end of a brick tossed from a roof than get cooperation from the locals.' Chigorin shrugs and smiles a what-can-ya-do? smile. Life is hard and you know what happens next. 'So, anyway, down to business. I'm here about your cellphone. You do own a cellphone, right?'

'Yes, but I almost never use it. My children live far away and I don't get out much.' Cole's smile is rueful. This is the first time he's shown any emotion and the Russian is quick to note it.

'Do you live here alone?'

'Essentially. I have a cleaning crew in twice a week. They handle my laundry as well.'

'You cook for yourself?'

'Simple things, chops, steaks, eggs.' He purses his lips for a moment, the gesture opaque, then continues. 'There was a time when my wife and I were avid readers of the restaurant reviews in the *New York Times*. Each year, we had at least one meal at every four-star restaurant in the city. Of course, we lived in Manhattan, then, and it was much easier to get around.' Another pursing of the lips, this time prolonged. 'Funny how the little bits of your life slip away. There's no trauma to it, only a day and a night and everything's changed.'

Chigorin thinks it over for a minute, then says, 'Actually, with my personal life, it's been more like a big explosion from day one. But about your cellphone. Does anyone besides you have authority to use it?'

'As I said, I live alone.'

244

'So, it's just you,' Chigorin persists. 'No-body else.'

'No.'

'What about without your knowledge?'

'I don't know what to say. My cellphone is on a bureau in my bedroom, plugged into the charger. Somebody on the cleaning crew might have used it, I suppose. I don't follow them about.' Cole pauses long enough to display a whip-crack of a smile. 'In fact, I try to keep out of their way.'

'I see. So when did you last use your phone? Do you remember?'

When Cole leans back his jaw comes up to shield his eyes. As if the lids weren't protection enough. 'Last week,' he says. 'I carried the phone on a visit to my ophthalmologist. But I didn't use it. In fact, I can't remember when I used it last.'

'Do you have a bill lying around some-where?'

Cole's mouth turns down, a smiley-face in reverse. 'No, I'm sorry. I pay my bills as soon as I get them and I don't keep the invoices. My cancelled check is proof of payment. I suppose I could phone my car-rier.'

'Or you could go online.'

'Yes, that would do it, too.'

Chigorin finishes his Coke, hands Cole a business card and struggles to his feet. 'I'd appreciate a call if you get around to it,' he says. 'If somebody cloned your cellphone, which happens every day, a record of his calls will show up on your bill. Of course, I could go to your carrier. But that would take weeks and the offense under investigation is very serious.' He limps toward the door, the pain in his ankle so ferocious he's imagining himself being fitted for a prosthesis.

'I almost forgot,' he says when they reach the door, 'I need the name of that cleaning company, and the names of any employees who had access to your cellphone.'

Cole flashes another quick grin. 'The company is called Paragon Cleaning Services. It's located in Greenpoint and the owners are Polish.'

'What about the workers? Are they Polish, too?'

'Yes, and they're very hard workers. Another reason I keep out of their way.'

NINETEEN

Hootie doesn't have a clue, not a glimmer, not a glimmer of a glimmer. He's been in a fog since Sherman Cole announced that his name was Sherman Cole. And the cop's not helping. He's limping along the path toward the car and he's frowning when he says, out of the corner of his mouth, 'Could you at least try to look casual, for Christ's sake?'

'What are you talkin' about?'

Chigorin manages to get halfway into the car, then has to raise his left leg with both hands and carry it inside before he closes the door. 'I'm startin' to lose patience, Hootie,' he says.

'Say again?'

'Get in the fuckin' car or I'll leave ya here.'

Chigorin's makes a U-turn the instant Hootie complies. He drives back to the Cross Island Parkway, but instead of returning to the city, heads out to Long Island, again running ten miles an hour above the speed limit. Hootie buckles up, then asks, 'Ya wanna tell me where we're goin'?'

'To a hospital. I gotta get this ankle checked out.'

'Now?'

Chigorin doesn't answer the question. Instead, he shakes his head in disgust and says, 'I shoulda killed the fuckin' dog. I'm talkin' about the little terrier that bit me. What is it the Dog Whisperer says? Rules, boundaries and limitations? I shoulda limited that mutt's boundaries by putting a bullet in his goddamned head.'

They're traveling alongside a bay – the one, Hootie assumes, Bayside is named after. There are sailors here, too, taking advantage of the gusty breeze. One boat in particular, bearing a crimson sail, is heeled over so far it appears about to capsize.

'So, that's it for Amelia,' Hootie says, more to himself than Chigorin.

'Not necessarily.'

'Not necessarily?'

'Hey, were you in that house with me? Did I hallucinate you?'

Finally, Hootie looses his temper. 'Fuck you, cop. I don't need to hear this bullshit.'

'But bullshit is exactly what you heard. Every word out of Cole's mouth was bullshit. It was an act, and a pretty bad one. Take this as gospel, Hootie, that asshole's dirty. And by the way, we only have his word that he's Sherman Cole. He didn't show ID.'

Hootie looks down at his hands. He'd swallowed every word Cole spoke, swallowed them whole. Now he doesn't know where to begin. Finally, he says, 'We were only there for ten minutes.'

'And half of that was waitin' for Cole to fetch our sodas. Which, by the way, you should've drank. But that's actually good, that you sat there like a lump.'

'Why?'

'Because Sherman Cole never asked who you were.'

'He probably thought I was your partner.'

'Gimme a break, Hootie. You're too young to be a cop, much less a detective. Cole should've asked, but he didn't. Just like he didn't ask us what we wanted, like I had to introduce the subject myself. I've knocked on hundreds of doors and I'm tellin ya, when they don't ask what you want it's because they already know. And by the way, he never asked what his cellphone was being used for either. That's a red flag right there. If someone was using your cellphone illegally, wouldn't you want to know what for?'

Again, Hootie's struck dumb, this time by the fact that he was such a dummy. He says nothing as the cop whips across traffic to catch the on-ramp to the eastbound Long Island Expressway.

'There's more, if ya wanna hear.'

'Why not?'

Predictably, Chigorin ignores the sarcasm. 'You told me the first phone contacts with the pedophile occurred a month ago.'

'More like six weeks.'

'In which case Mr. Cole paid a bill that reflects those calls, right? So why didn't he notice them? Keep in mind, he told us that he almost never uses the phone. That means his bills should be the same, month after month.'

'Maybe he just pays the bills without checking. He's pretty far out of it.'

'Hootie, did you notice those glass-fronted cabinets on the wall behind Cole's chair? I mean, you had plenty of time to look around while he was in the kitchen.' Chigorin pauses, but Hootie doesn't reply. 'Well, one of them had little statues in it and the other had little boxes and there wasn't a speck of dust anywhere. The glass was clean, too, even at the edges. In fact, the whole room was spotless. So you can put aside Cole's act. He's not a poor broken-hearted widower. He's very much in control of his life. And you can forget what I said about cloning his cellphone, too. That didn't happen.'

'How do you know?'

'Cellphones transmit a radio signal to a cell tower, a signal that includes the phone's serial number. That's how your carrier knows who to bill for the call. What cloners do is intercept the signal, then program your serial number into another cellphone. It's no big deal. All you need is a scanner and a lot of patience. But you can't intercept a signal if the phone isn't being used.'

'What about the cleaning crew?'

'The Polish cleaning crew? The crew that doesn't speak English? Look, you can pick apart any of the points I made, but not all of them. That prick is dirty and I plan to fuck him over. I just can't figure out how.'

Chigorin exits the Expressway at Lakeville Road. He makes a quick right, drives past a golf course and a small lake, finally turns in to Long Island Jewish Hospital's emergency entrance. There's a security guard standing outside the emergency room door. He's smoking a cigarette and he approaches the car before it even comes to a stop.

'You can't park here.'

Chigorin flashes his shield as he opens the door. He has to get both his feet on to the pavement, then put all his weight on his right foot before he can stand.

'I gotta see someone about my ankle,' he tells the guard.

Hootie comes around the car and takes Chigorin's arm. By now, he's thinking of the cop as a force of nature. You don't play his game, he takes his ball and goes home.

'Well, leave the keys in case I have to move the car.'

'They're in the ignition.'

With Hootie's assistance, Chigorin limps into the emergency room and up to the intake window. The nurse on the other side of a wide counter glances at his badge and smiles. She's a dark-skinned black woman with a round face and a narrow, fleshy mouth.

'My husband's on the job,' she says.

Chigorin returns her smile. 'I got bit on the ankle two days ago and now I'm swollen up. And there's pus, too. I gotta get the wound cleaned out.'

'Bitten by a dog?'

'Yeah, a little one.'

'They're the worst. Their teeth make puncture wounds that close up when they let go, trapping bacteria. Two days later you have an infection.'

'Yeah, that's it exactly. The problem is that I'm on the clock right now, so I need to get out in a hurry. This investigation I'm workin', it's a kidnapping. I mean of a kid, too, a twelve-year-old girl.'

Her maternal instincts properly stoked, the nurse straightens. 'Don't worry, we're not that busy. I should be able to speed up the process. Lemme have your insurance card.'

Ten minutes later, Hootie and Chigorin are inside a private cubicle usually reserved for patients with infectious diseases. There's a gurney in the room, along with a heart monitor, a blood pressure cuff and an empty IV stand. A dispenser on the wall holds boxes of vinyl gloves. Chigorin's sitting on the edge of the gurney, reaching for the knot on his left shoelace, but he's not having much luck. Hootie lets him struggle for minute, then says, 'You need some help, Detective?'

Unable to raise his foot to meet his hands, Chigorin jerks forward and snatches at the lace. He succeeds in untying the knot, but the shoe remains firmly on his foot.

'Fuck it,' he says. 'Leave it for the nurse. That's why she makes the big bucks.'

Hootie takes Chigorin's foot and eases the shoe off. He's about to do the same with the cop's sock, but then notices that the sock is wet. He doesn't know what the moisture is, only that he doesn't want to touch it.

'You figure it out yet?' he asks.

'Figure out what?' Chigorin lays down on the gurney.

'What you're gonna do about Amelia.'

'No.'

'Well, if it's nothin', tell me now.'

'Why? So you can go back there? Force your way inside?'

'Something like that.'

'First thing, you don't even know if she's there. I mean, she could be. There's an attached garage with an automatic door –

that'd make it easy to get her inside. But she doesn't have to be.'

'Wait a second. How do you know the garage has an automatic door?'

'Because there's no handle or lock on the outside, which is something you might've noticed when we pulled up.'

Hootie sits down on the edge of the bed. He's thinking the keys are in the car. All he has to do is walk out the door and offer to move it for the security guard. He's thinking maybe the cop doesn't have all that many cards to play.

'Do me a favor, don't talk down to me,' he says. 'I'm not your dog.'

'OK, I apologize. But you need to think a little bit. Like, how did the chicken hawk move Amelia from that apartment into his car?' Chigorin answers the question without pausing. 'He put a gun to her head, that's how. The same gun that'll be put to your head if you try to force your way in there. Now my problem is that I don't have probable cause for a search, with or without a warrant. I'm operating on gut instinct and nothin' I find inside that house will be admissible in a court of law. So if Amelia's dead and we find her body, her killers are gonna walk.'

The admissibility of evidence being a topic in which he's supremely uninterested, Hootie simply tunes out. The gun strapped to his ankle seems heavier now. He imagines it tucked beneath his waistband as he approaches Cole's house. According to Chigorin, Hootie's too young to be a cop and Sherman Cole must know it. Would that also render Hootie unthreatening? Would Cole hesitate long enough for Hootie to put the .38 in his face and cock the hammer? Hootie represses a smile, again recalling the many times Bubba pitched him. Despite his prison record, Bubba never came off as threatening, not once. In fact, he was a model of gentle persuasion. A weaver of dreams.

What's the expression? Trick me once, shame on you? Trick me twice, shame on me? Hootie's thinking that from the minute he entered the subway station, his whole life's been a trick. And he's not free yet. Some part of his brain still hopes to put everything back together. Or maybe not his brain. Hootie's thoughts have turned to the little Asian girl he met in the club. And yeah, he wants that, too.

Hootie's reverie is interrupted by the entrance of a nurse, an R.N. named Arroyo, according to the ID pinned to her uniform. A tiny woman with the doe eyes and small flat nose of a Filipina, she pulls two gloves from one of the boxes on the wall and slides them over her hands. 'Shall we take a look?' she asks.

Chigorin levers himself up to a sitting position. 'You might wanna go easy there,' he cautions.

Arroyo slides the sock over the Russian's ankle. 'Have you had a tetanus shot?'

'Yes.'

'Are you taking antibiotics?'

The Russian winces when Arroyo lifts the tape holding the dressing in place. But the wet tape and the wetter dressing pull off easily. The ankle beneath is slick with yellow pus and obviously swollen, while the flesh surrounding the two puncture wounds is red enough to make Chigorin flinch.

'Are you taking antibiotics?' the nurse repeats.

'I have a prescription, but I didn't fill it.'

Dr. Immanuel Branson chooses that moment to make an appearance. He's a kid, maybe in his late twenties, with rumpled hair and half-moons the color of wet tea bags beneath his eyes. He introduces himself, shakes the Russian's hand, then says, 'I'm afraid we're going to have to excise that wound, Detective.'

'Excise?'

'I'll make a small incision at each puncture, then manually clean the wound. But don't worry. An injection will take care of the pain. You won't feel anything.'

'That's what I'm afraid of.'

'I don't understand.'

'If I get my ankle numbed, will I be able to walk?'

'Well enough to get home if you're reasonably careful.'

'But I should avoid chasing perps through dark alleyways?'

'Absolutely.'

'And what if I don't take the injection?'

'In that case, it'll only be a matter of dealing with the pain.'

Chigorin draws a long breath, then looks up at Hootie. 'You wanna do me a favor, kid? Go wait by the car.'

'You're kicking me out?'

'Yeah.'

'What did I do?'

'You didn't do anything, Hootie. I just don't want you to see me cry.'

TWENTY

Forty-five minutes later, his face the color of wet cigarette ash, Chigorin limps into the parking lot. Despite an ordeal that's left him weak and nauseated, his ankle feels a lot better than it did when he walked through the emergency room door. The swelling is down, the pressure on the nerves greatly reduced. The Russian may not be prepared to run a hundred-yard dash, but he doesn't feel like he's about to fall over when he puts his left foot on the ground. Plus, according to Branson, the Russian's head wound is healing up nicely. The headache he's been suffering all day has vanished.

Chigorin spots Hootie standing next to the car. He feels a momentary compassion for the kid. Talk about in over your head. The Russian recalls an encounter with an emotionally disturbed prize fighter, way back when he was a gung-ho rookie on foot patrol. Against the advice of his partner, he had approached the fighter, intending to 'talk him down'. One little problem, though. The man didn't want to be talked down. He was off his meds and wanted to kick some cop ass. The punches came so quick, and from so many directions, Chigorin felt like he was being attacked by a mob.

'Everything cool?' Hootie asks.

'Never better. You ready?'

'For what?'

'We're goin' back to Cole's. I'm gonna describe the investigation, taking care to emphasize the damsel in distress part, then ask for permission to search the house. Just so we can eliminate him as a suspect.'

'What if he says no?'

Chigorin's reaching for the vodka before he shuts the car door. He drinks greedily, with his eyes closed, a baby at the tit. 'Fuck me,' he mutters as he caps the bottle, then starts the car.

'Let's suppose,' he tells Hootie, 'that Sherman Cole's exactly what he appears to be. A retired widower victimized by someone who either cloned his cellphone or used it without his permission. Wouldn't you expect him to be moved by the plight of a kidnapped little girl? Wouldn't you expect him to cooperate? I mean, we're only tryin' to clear him, right? And it's not like we're gonna conduct a close search, like we're gonna look through his drawers or examine his computer.'

'So, if he refuses, then you'll do the search?'

'Actually, I'm gonna toss the house whether he likes it or not. But I wanna see how he reacts first.'

In the silence that follows, the Russian finds himself recharging. The booze, probably. But he's thinking clearly now. Sherman Cole has put himself in a bind. He's established himself as a sad sack widower. He can't suddenly become the outraged libertarian protecting his right to privacy. Not without giving the game away. Chigorin's only regret is that he didn't reach this conclusion while he was still at the house, a failure he blames on his injured ankle. The pain had been so bad, he could not focus on anything else. He kept imagining a doc sayin': 'Of course, we'll have to take the leg.'

The Russian's clear thinking extends to the warning he gave to Hootie. Beware of kidnappers with guns. If the house contains evidence of Amelia's fate, there's every reason to expect a violent response to a forced search. Especially if Amelia's already dead. Back in Manhattan, he might convince a buddy to cover him while he conducted an illegal search. But not in the 111th Precinct where he doesn't know a soul. There's just him and Hootie.

Chigorin would like to be rid of Hootie, but that's not possible. If the man who kidnapped Amelia is in the house, Chigorin needs Hootie to make an identification. That way he can invent some bullshit about seeing the man through a window, or maybe claim the man was standing behind Cole when Cole opened the door. But that's for later. For now, the situation facing him is extremely simple. There's a citizen in need of immediate aid and he's the only one who can aid her and he's a cop. Case fucking closed.

Surprisingly, Chigorin had come to this conclusion while Dr. Branson was cleaning out his wound. The pain was beyond anything he'd ever experienced. And yes, the tears did flow. Yet somehow, along the way, he became resigned. He couldn't back off. Not after all the years in Homicide. There were just too many bodies, too many innocent bystanders, too many grieving families. Notifying those families, watching their lives fall apart, bearing witness to their loss, that was always the worst part. The wailing and the gnashing of teeth.

Chigorin takes another drink, a parting shot, so to speak. He's parked in front of Sherman Cole's stately mock-Tudor home, admiring a neatly-trimmed hedge. The hedge is so thick, the top so flat, it appears to be a single plant.

'Alright,' Hootie says, 'so how do you wanna play it?'

'Apologetic. We're sorry to bother you again, we know it's an inconvenience, do you mind if we come inside for a moment? And I wanna maintain that tone until he answers the million dollar question.'

'You're giving him every chance to do the right thing.'

'Hootie, that's it exactly. That's my modus operandi. Talk nice. Save the threats for when you really need 'em.' Chigorin removes the keys from the ignition and slides them into his pocket. 'But I do have one problem.'

'What?'

'Well, I can justify conducting an illegal search to my bosses, even if the evidence is thrown out of court. But what I can't justify is taking a civilian into a life-threatening situation. Now I need you here in case the man you saw in Washington Square happens to be in the house. I need you to make an identification, which is why I brought you along in the first place.'

'Yeah, so?'

'So, you're gonna stay in the car until I finish the search.'

Hootie laughs. What he's feeling, mainly, is relief. He's done it. Despite all his doubts. He's going to find Amelia, one way or the other. And when he thinks about it, his doubts were definitely grounded. Without the cop, he'd never have seen through Cole's bullshit. No, he'd have backed away, made his apologies, driven off, given up. He'd have sent Bubba to jail for nothing.

Hootie opens the door. 'I'm goin' in, with you or without you,' he announces.

'I knew you'd say that, Hootie. But one thing you might wanna think about. Failing to obey a lawful order from a police officer is a crime. I can arrest you here and now.'

'Not without shooting me you can't.'

Hootie's not exactly bluffing, but he steps out of the car before Chigorin can grab him. There's nothing to be gained by fighting cops. Chigorin follows, though it takes him longer to gain his feet.

'Can you at least keep your mouth shut and let me do the talking?'

'Yeah, absolutely.' Hootie's surprised by how easily the lie flows from his mouth. It's almost like someone else is speaking, an actor reciting a piece of dialogue. He gestures to Cole's front door. 'Ready when you are,' he says.

They walk up the path side by side, Chigorin limping along, Hootie's stride tense. Though both steal a sidelong glance at the leaded windows, all seems in order until they're within a few feet of the double doors. Then Chigorin notices that the door on the right is open. Not much, just a fraction of an inch.

Chigorin gives the door a little push, allowing in enough light to reveal a cluster of red stains on the foyer's stone floor. The stains are droplets and perfectly round. They could only have been created by blood dripping from a stationary human being.

Hootie watches Chigorin draw his 9 mm Glock. The sight of the weapon shocks him and he becomes acutely aware of the .38 strapped to his ankle. He even considers pulling it. But no, not yet. In New York City, possession of an illegal handgun carries a minimum, mandatory sentence of three and a half years. Better to stay cool for the present.

Chigorin turns to Hootie, but Hootie merely shakes his head. 'Forget the lecture,' he tells the cop. 'I'm goin' in, with you or without you.'

Navigating the blood trail in the house doesn't require the expertise of a Navajo tracker. The drops form a gentle arc, crossing the living room and the kitchen to the head of a stairway that drops into a shadowy basement. There are shoe impressions in the blood, smears mostly, but Chigorin's pretty sure the impressions were left coming and going. He flicks the light switch, but is not surprised when the basement remains dark.

'Police,' he bellows. 'Is anyone down there?' He pauses briefly, then adds, 'Police. I'm coming down.'

Hootie feels his heart jump in his chest

when the Russian begins to descend. Something's stirring in his gut, something beyond emotion, or even sensation, though not at all unpleasant. There's blood on the floor and whoever left it is in that basement. Maybe dead or dying. Or maybe laying in wait, the monster in the closet. Twice, Hootie's been caught in shoot-outs, both times an innocent bystander. He didn't panic, diving to the ground on each occasion. But his hands shook for ninety minutes afterward.

Stay cool, he tells himself as he takes the first step. Stay cool, little brother.

At the bottom of the stairs, Chigorin's not feeling much more confident than Hootie. He's facing a corridor with darkened rooms on either side. The only light fills a doorway at the end of the corridor, perhaps sixty feet away.

'Police,' he repeats, this time even louder. 'Is anyone back there?' His voice echoes in the confined space, seeming to mock him. What he needs – what he knows he needs – is a squad to clear the darkened rooms. But that's not going to happen. There's just him and the kid and the light at the end of the tunnel.

'Wait here until I check the side rooms,' he

tells Hootie. 'And don't give me a hard time.'

But Hootie's seeing exactly what Chigorin's seeing and the last thing he wants is to be the first one to walk the length of that corridor. 'Yeah, go ahead. You're the one with the gun.'

TWENTY-ONE

Chigorin begins with a simple choice. Fifteen feet away, a pair of doors lead into a pair of rooms, one to the Russian's left and one to his right. He can't search either room without exposing his back to someone lurking in the other. This is not the way cops do it, except when an emergency situation, like a clear blood trail, demands immediate action. So Chigorin takes a step, then another, eyes flicking from left to right as he tries to make up his mind. Door number one or door number two? Make a mistake and Sherman Cole or his partner takes your head off. Make a mistake and your daughter gets to attend your funeral.

But Chigorin does make a mistake, two in fact. Although he guesses correctly, choosing the door to his right, his mind is divided, his attention more on his uncovered back than the task at hand. As a result, he comes too far into the room and is taken by surprise. His second mistake is immediately apparent. The individual standing to the right of the door, the individual who jams the barrel of an automatic into his ribs, is not a man, or even a woman. She's a girl, at least in appearance, and while not technically a 'good guy', certainly a victim. Her left eye is black and rapidly swelling. A makeshift bandage, blood-soaked, encases her left hand. Her blouse is plastered to her back, so tight the lacerations beneath are plainly visible.

'You wanna live?' Amelia asks.

'Hey, I'm a cop. I'm not here to hurt you.' Chigorin's voice is soothing, or as soothing as he can make it with his heart pounding away hard enough to crack his ribs.

Amelia's weapon doesn't move, as the tension in her voice doesn't diminish. 'I asked you if you want to live.'

'Yeah, as a matter of fact, I do.'

'Then be a good boy.'

Amelia's bandaged left hand grasps Chigorin's right hand, the one holding his Glock. Slowly and very deliberately, her fingers slide up to grip the barrel, leaving a blood trail behind. Then Chigorin's weapon is in her hand and she's prodding him back into the hallway.

'Where's Bubba?' she asks.

Hootie's standing there, holding on to the .38, which he drew at the sound of Amelia's voice. Try as he might, he can't wrap his mind around her appearance. His eyes jump from the black eye to the bloody hand to the wounds on her back, never stopping long enough to absorb the facts. Not that he's especially afraid – if there's any threat, it's to the cop, who's staring at the .38 as though Hootie conjured it out of thin air.

'Hootie, you breathing or what? Where's Bubba?'

'Busted.'

'On what charge?'

'Parole violation, but they're lookin' at him for a murder.'

'Is this guy really a cop?'

'Yeah.'

Chigorin picks that moment to try again. He doesn't care for the gun in his ribs, but as it doesn't waver and Amelia's blue eyes betray more than a measure of madness, he doesn't try to move it away.

'Hey,' he says, his tone eminently reasonable, 'I'm the good guy. I'm here to help you. At considerable risk to myself, lemme add.'

Amelia ignores his plea. 'We're gonna walk into the room in front of you, the room with the light. There are two men in there, one alive and one dead. I want you to go sit by the live one. You do anything else, anything at all, without doubt I'm gonna shoot you.'

'Amelia, he's right,' Hootie says. 'It's all over.'

But Amelia doesn't as much as glance in Hootie's direction. She steps back, leveling the gun on Chigorin's spine. 'I don't like cops, so don't give me an excuse,' she announces. 'Get moving.'

As he watches Amelia and Chigorin disappear into the room, Hootie remembers the first time he walked into a Rikers Island housing area. Christ, but he'd been scared. Talk about suck-it-up time. Show fear and you'd be wearing lipstick by morning. He touches the .38's cylinder to his temple as he follows Amelia, telling himself to stay cool, stay cool, stay cool.

Hootie stops in the doorway, despite the effort to steel himself. There's a body to his left, the body of the man who passed himself off as Sherman Cole. His eye has been pierced with a narrow shard of wood torn from the frame of a closet door. Hootie estimates the shard to be eight inches long, though he can't be sure how much of it is buried inside the man's brain.

The real Sherman Cole is sitting on the floor at the far end of the room, his hands cuffed to a pipe behind his back. His mouth has been duct-taped, the tape passing several times around his head. Yet he appears, with his veiled eyes and shovel chin, somehow at ease.

Chigorin's sitting beside Cole, as ordered. His legs are stretched out before him, most likely because of his ankle. But it's now impossible for him to move fast, no matter what the provocation. And Amelia hasn't lowered the barrel of the Glock. She's fifteen feet away, perched on the edge of a queen-sized bed, staring at Cole and Chigorin. Above her, a bank of lights hanging from a metal frame complements a trio of video cameras lined up against the wall behind the dead man. There are mic stands and microphones as well, and an array of children's clothing on a metal rack. In the corner, to Hootie's left, a cast-iron safe rises to a height of four feet. The safe is old and dirty, the dial pocked with rust.

'Rip the tape off his mouth,' Amelia tells Chigorin. 'Let's see what Shermie has to say.'

Chigorin takes his time, removing the tape slowly and gently. A small act of defiance? Hootie's not sure. He's positioned himself to Amelia's left behind the bed.

'Is that how you hurt your hand?' Chigorin nods toward the body. 'Ripping that wood off the closet?'

Amelia doesn't reply. Her eyes are fixed on Sherman Cole. And he's staring back at her through the slits between his eyelids. His tongue criss-crosses his lips, back and forth, until he finally spits out a bit of duct tape.

'You shouldn't have returned,' he complains to Chigorin. 'You've only made the bargaining process more complicated.'

'Bargaining? For what?' Chigorin asks.

'My miserable life, of course.'

'Your life? I can't even count the crimes you've committed, or the years you can expect to spend in prison. Your life is over, you freak.'

'Enough,' Amelia says. She produces a handcuff key and tosses it to Chigorin. 'Uncuff him.'

But the Russian hasn't had enough, and Hootie suddenly realizes that Chigorin is also bargaining for his life. That's because he knows that Amelia can't murder Sherman Cole and leave a cop around to tell the tale. No, that wouldn't do at all. Hootie watches Chigorin remove Cole's handcuffs, all the while thinking, And what about Hootie Two-Bears Hootier?

Cole rubs at the red streaks encircling his wrists. 'Thank you, Veronica. Now, where were we?'

'You were offering me a bribe.'

'A bribe? No, that's too harsh, my dear. I believe I was attempting to make a down payment on my life. What would it take to convince you to forget, if not forgive?'

'You hear that, Hootie?' Amelia asks without turning around.

'Yeah, I hear it.'

'So whatta ya think? How high's the moon?'

Hootie steps backward and to his right. He's now standing directly behind Amelia on the far side of the bed. 'I think you need to end this. Nobody's gonna blame you for what happened to...'

'To Brian Moore? That's his real name.

And, oh, thank you.'

'For what?'

Amelia responds without turning away from Chigorin and Cole. 'For showing up before. You created a distraction and they left me alone for a few minutes. Big mistake, Hootie. Big fuckin' mistake. Only you shouldn't have come back.' She pauses long enough to draw a breath, then gestures to Cole. 'Open the safe.'

'Yes, of course. But you do understand, what's in this safe is merely cash on hand. There's a good deal more to be had. Consider this home, for instance, paid for long ago. Even now, in a depressed market, it's worth upwards of two million dollars.'

'Unlock the safe, pull the door open and back away. If your hand goes inside, I promise you, Shermie, it'll never come out.'

Hootie watches Cole traverse the room on his hands and knees. As far as he can tell, the man appears unafraid. Cole's playing the only card in his deck and he's prepared to accept the consequences. The same cannot be said of Chigorin. The cop's eyes dart around the room until they finally settle on Hootie's. Is there a plea in that look? Or a set of instructions? Chigorin's eyes move away before Hootie can decide.

'Now, I must warn you, Veronica. You may be shocked by what's in the safe. I mean besides the money. Please don't do anything rash.'

Cole twirls the dial, left, then right, then left again. He yanks the handle down and pulls the door open before settling back on his heels. 'The money's in the box.'

In fact, a gray metal box, perhaps eight inches deep and ten inches high, rests on the topmost shelf. But that's not what catches Hootie's eye. Besides the box, the entire safe is filled with DVDs. Hootie does not have to ask what's on those DVDs. Nobody locks *Gone with the Wind* in a safe. Still, Chigorin poses a question.

'What's that,' the cop asks, 'your sales catalog?'

'We never forced anyone to do anything.' Cole sniffs defiantly. 'We recruited the willing and we paid them well.'

Chigorin glances at Amelia, then says, 'Willing? Gimme a break. Ya know, short-eyes don't do well in prison. They tend to be victimized by the other inmates, so they naturally ask for protective custody, which is nothing more than solitary confinement.

What that means, Sherman, is that you're gonna spend twenty-three hours a day in a six-by-ten-foot cell for the rest of your life.'

Another plea, but Amelia's not listening. 'How much?' she asks Cole.

'A bit more than thirty thousand dollars.'

Amelia laughs. 'You remember what Bubba said, Hootie?'

'Give me three thousand and I'll turn it into thirty thousand. Give me thirty, I'll turn it into three hundred. Yeah, I remember.'

Amelia lays the Glock on the bed and picks up Chigorin's nine millimeter, also a Glock. 'How bad is it?' she asks. 'For Bubba?'

'I don't know. I'm not a lawyer.'

'You snitch him out?'

'Yeah. I told them he killed the rat in the subway. But they don't have the gun and I'm the only witness.'

'And this cop here, he's the one who collared Bubba?'

'He was just doing his job, Amelia. And Bubba, he slipped the keys to the apartment into my pocket. He wanted me to talk.'

'And why is that?'

'So I could ride to your fucking rescue.'

Amelia hesitates for a fraction of a second, then addresses Cole. 'Tell me about the movies.'

'Certainly, but first let me say that what's happened to you isn't typical. When Brian discovered that you were recording his ... his visit? Well, I'm afraid Brian wasn't the sharpest pencil in the box. He overreacted and brought you here, much to my dismay. If he'd left, then and there, we wouldn't be in this mess.'

Amelia shakes her head. 'Tell me about the movies,' she repeats. 'Where did you get your little actresses? Or were there little actors, too?'

'Really, Veronica, there's a police officer present. I don't...' Cole freezes when Amelia draws the Glock's hammer back. His eyes jam shut and he raises his shoulders defensively. Still, he manages to speak.

'We recruit girls online, as we might eventually have recruited you, and also through a ... a network of friends. As I said, there's no force involved. The girls are paid and paid well. If you were to watch any of the videos, you'd see that right away. The girls are eager, they're smiling.'

Amelia's left eye is now swollen shut, her

depth perception severely impaired. But the loss of binocular vision doesn't affect her aim when she pulls the trigger. The bullet strikes Cole in the center of his face, passing through his brain in an almost straight line before tearing out the back of his head.

The roar of the gun in the windowless room is loud enough to obliterate thought and the only moving thing, for a long moment, is Sherman Cole's body folding gently on itself before toppling to the side. Amelia stares at Cole as though expecting him to rise. When he remains motionless, despite the blood pooling around his face, her eyes turn to Chigorin. The Glock's muzzle begins to follow an instant later, but Hootie's prepared this time. He cocks the .38 to draw her attention.

'No way,' he says. 'Put the gun down.'

Amelia's arm stops, but she holds on to the weapon. 'Anybody else know you're here?' she asks.

'Uh-uh.'

'Then why not? Ya know we're gonna need money to find a lawyer for Bubba. Otherwise, he'll get a Legal Aid jerk with two hundred clients.'

'That's Bubba's problem. He knew what he was doing.'

'Easy for you to say.'

'Easy because it's the truth. Bubba was my partner. I'm sorry for what happened to him, but it was mostly his own fault and I'm not gonna kill a cop to protect him.'

'Good thinking, but it doesn't work that way for me. That's because the story I told you before left something out. Bubba's not my partner, he's my stepbrother. Now, I don't wanna bore you with the sad details of my early years, but by the time our mother died, when I was eight, both our fathers were long gone. Bubba, he was just startin' out at St. Johns, playin' ball and tryin' to keep his grades up. Nobody would've blamed him if he cut me loose, but he didn't. He busted his ass all day and came home at night to make sure I had clean clothes and something to eat. And he kept on doin' it until the day he was sentenced. That's gotta be worth more than a kiss-off. More than, "It's mostly his own fault."'

Hootie wills himself to remain alert. Amelia's voice is softening and she's becoming somehow younger, while he seems to be going in the opposite direction, adding years.

He tells himself not to pity her, to forget the eye and the wounds on her back, forget her whole life. He's no more to blame for Amelia's suffering than for Bubba killing the rat. What's happening here is about survival and he has a right to survive.

'Mother dead,' Amelia continued. 'Father missing. No relatives. Hootie, believe me when I tell ya that foster care is a real crapshoot. There are good foster homes out there. I know from talkin' to other foster kids. But there are bad ones out there, too, and I landed in every one of 'em. Funny thing, though, when Bubba made parole and we got back together, he never cut me any slack on account of what happened to me. Not for the Kallmann syndrome, either. He told me about a fighter named Joe Frazier who once beat Muhammad Ali. Frazier had a motto: "Whenever you get knocked down, in or out of the ring, stand up and fire back."'

Amelia's voice finally trails off and her chin falls slightly. For a moment Hootie thinks she's going to put the gun down. But when she snaps back to attention, he's the first to speak.

'You murder a cop,' he tells her, 'they

never stop lookin' for you. And when they find you, if they don't kill you on the spot, they put you away forever. I'm nineteen, Amelia. I don't wanna die in a cell. Keep in mind, your DNA's all over the house.'

Amelia lets her hand fall into her lap, though her forefinger continues to rest on the Glock's trigger. 'You know what we were up to, the point of the exercise?' she asks Chigorin. 'Did Hootie shoot off his mouth about that, too?'

The question stirs Chigorin. He's sitting with his back against the wall ten feet away, completely helpless. 'Nobody's gonna hold you accountable for what happened here,' he tells her. 'Cops hate pedophiles, especially cops who have daughters, like me.'

'And what about the extortion? You gonna forget about that, too? And what about pretending to be twelve when I'm really nineteen? What happens after my computer's examined and they find all those emails? And what happens when the reporters dig into the story? And what about the money? 'Cause I'm tellin' ya, after everything that's happened, I feel I'm entitled to compensation. Otherwise, it was all for nothin'.'

Chigorin responds without hesitation, the

stakes obvious to him and everyone else in the room. 'Hootie was right, Amelia. Your DNA's gonna be found in this house. There's no cleaning up.'

'So what? My DNA's not on file anywhere. And recovering my DNA only means that I was present at some unknown point. It doesn't mean I pulled the trigger.' This time, when Chigorin begins to speak, she cuts him off.

'Bubba thought a lot of you, Hootie,' she declares. 'He said you had undeveloped talent. Seriously, man. He said your only problem was that you were still looking for yourself. I didn't argue with him because there was no point. When Bubba makes up his mind, he's got a head like a rock. But I always wondered, Hootie, which way you'd go if you were squeezed.'

Amelia jerks her chin in Chigorin's direction. 'Cops are paid to lie. They lie all the time. That's why Bubba went to jail. They told him it looked like a clear case of self-defense and they only wanted to hear his side of the story. Then they charged him with murder. You understand what I'm sayin', right? We let this cop walk away, we're both goin' to prison.'

When Hootie finally admits the obvious – he's going to have to kill Amelia to stop her – something inside him slips away. A barrier of sorts. His past, his heritage, has finally become irrelevant. There's only now. There's only what he does or doesn't do right this minute. And he can't wait for Amelia to make the first move and hope he reacts fast enough. No, the worst outcome he can imagine is being in this room with four bodies and no witnesses. He might as well put the .38 to his head and make it five.

'Let go of the gun,' he tells Amelia. But his finger's already tightening on the .38's trigger. He's out of words and now it's a matter of will. He orders himself to squeeze down, but he can't. He can't and he can't and he can't. And then he does.

TWENTY-TWO

Hootie steps into a pair of wool slacks and pulls them on. He zips up and fastens the top button, finally slips a braided belt through the loops. Though he's worn the slacks before, he can't get used to how soft they are. His prior experience with woolen garments has been limited to the itchy suits he wore to church. At his mom's insistence, of course. These slacks, a wool–silk blend, are as soft as velvet. And they fit him perfectly, falling in a straight line to the tops of the tasseled loafers he steps into.

As he often does these days, Hootie pauses to examine himself in a full-length mirror on the back of a closet door. He's been working out three times a week for the past month and it's beginning to show. His chest and abs are sharply defined, his shoulders rounded. When he finally pulls a silk T-shirt over his head and tucks it into his trousers, his torso divides into a series of planes, though the charcoal T-shirt is not at all tight.

Hootie runs his fingers through his hair. Inky black and thick, it curls to the tops of his ears, complementing a deep tan. These days, he's getting second looks from women who wouldn't give him a first look when he was a confused teenager named Hootie Hootier. Back before he transformed himself into Judson Two-Bears Hootier, multiracial and proud of it.

Anyone you wanna be, he tells himself. That's his mantra, now. Say it and say it again, until you finally believe it.

Hootie completes his outfit by slipping into a suede jacket. The gray jacket is rumpled by design, and it took Hootie a while to get used to the fit. Given its cost, he figured it should cling to his torso, a second skin. But he sees the point now and he's glad he took Pete's advice. This is New York. Tight-ass is for stock brokers and corporate lawyers, not young entrepreneurs with more balls than bankroll. Because that's what Hootie's become, or at least the part he's playing. Eager for risk, ready to throw those dice.

With a last glance, he walks to a window,

one of two in the tiny apartment. The window is open slightly and the draft on his face and his hands is noticeably cool. It's well into September now, nearly two months since the police discovered the bodies of Amelia Cincone, Brian Moore and Sherman Cole in a very fancy house in the very fancy neighborhood of Bayside Gables.

The house, the neighborhood and the white victims were enough, all by themselves, to excite the media vultures. But with no arrest for the homicides and the cops leaking tidbit after tidbit, the story simply exploded. The hidden room in the basement, the video equipment and the DVDs came first. Then the news that a joint NYPD–FBI team had broken the encryption on Cole's hard drive, yielding a treasure trove of names and addresses. Finally the biggest scoop of all when Amelia was tied to Bubba Yablonsky, now awaiting a parole hearing on Rikers Island. A columnist in the *Daily News* openly accused Bubba of pimping his stepsister.

Outside, the day has a picture-perfect feel to it. The sky is intensely blue, the small scudding clouds milky white. Scarlet at the edges, the leaves of a maple on the lawn are just beginning to turn. Hootie glances up the street, then crosses the room to the apartment's single upholstered chair. He sits down and picks up the storyboard lying on a table to his left. Hootie worked long and hard on the storyboard, blocking out the half-minute commercial almost second by second. Along the way, he discovered a minor talent for drawing and the storyboard has a professional feel to it. This is important because preparing the storyboard would cost thousands of dollars if they had to farm the job out. That's another lesson Hootie's absorbed as he read book after book on television marketing. Whenever possible, do it yourself.

But right this minute, Hootie's unable to concentrate. He closes the storyboard and walks back to the window. There are times, and this is one of them, when he can't sit still, when Amelia's quick grin and Bubba's relentless optimism whip through his consciousness, relentless as demons. Even as he pulls aside the curtains, some corner of his mind searches for alternatives. He and Bubba arriving before Cole's partner got Amelia out of the apartment. Amelia welcoming them as rescuers. Amelia giving up, lowering the gun.

Not that Hootie blames himself for what happened. No, to his way of thinking, Amelia and Bubba should have confirmed Cole's identity before moving forward. They'd gone so far as to photograph the house. They might have waited around long enough to discover who lived there. And there's something else, too, something Hootie discovered online. Kallmann syndrome can be treated with hormones. If Amelia still looked twelve after hooking up with Bubba, it's because she wanted to look twelve.

When Peter Chigorin's car enters the block, Hootie's thoughts flash back to Sherman Cole's basement, another post-traumatic tic. After pulling the trigger, he'd literally frozen. Not so the cop – or the ex-cop, now that he's retired. Chigorin was pressing his finger into Amelia's throat before the echoes died away, looking for a pulse that wasn't there. Then he retrieved his gun and the cartridge casing on the floor, and dug the bullet that went through Cole's head out of the wall. One, two, three. Like he'd plucked the sequence out of some training manual.

'You saved my life,' he told Hootie as he pocketed the shell casings, 'and I'm not forgettin'. I owe you forever.'

Kneeling on the bed, stunned, Hootie didn't resist when Chigorin took the .38, wiped it down and dropped it to the floor. Nor did he move when the cop pulled the metal box out of the safe and opened it to reveal stacks of banded hundreds and fifties, or when Chigorin transferred the money from the box to a camera bag. In fact, he might never have moved if Chigorin didn't force the issue.

'Time to go, Hootie.' The cop hadn't waited for Hootie to respond. He grabbed Hootie by the arm, yanked him to his feet, then dragged him down the hall and up the stairs to a window in the living room. Limping all the way. Outside, the sun had set and it was nearly dark. The street, for as far as Hootie could see, was deserted.

'What we're gonna do is walk out to the car, get in and drive away. Just like nothin' happened.'

'What about the shots?' Hootie finally rediscovered his voice. 'What if someone heard them?'

'Then we're fucked. But I don't think so.

You got a basement room with no windows, plus the walls are padded. That's why the shots were so loud. The sound was trapped inside. But, hey, you think about it, there's plenty that could still go wrong. Maybe somebody noticed us comin' in, maybe someone'll see us comin' out. Or maybe some dog walker noticed the car. What I'm hopin' is that the bodies won't be discovered for a few days. That'll make time of death hard to pin down.'

Hootie didn't speak on the drive back to Manhattan, not until Chigorin parked in front of Bubba's apartment house on the Lower East Side. At eight o'clock, the neighborhood was just getting into gear and the sidewalks were crowded. A group of smokers standing outside a bar spilled over the sidewalk, puffing away. Across the street, an enormous pit bull in a leather harness pulled a girl in a wheelchair toward First Avenue. Hootie tried to absorb what he saw, but he couldn't get his mind out of that basement. Amelia hadn't uttered a word, hadn't even groaned as she pitched forward. It was like she'd given up, like she was looking for a way out.

'Why are we here?' he asked the cop.

'You told me that you personally bought the surveillance cameras. That means you showed your face, right?'

'That's right.'

'Well, if there are any receipts, we need to destroy 'em. Same for any computer hard drives. And those Cookinarts?'

'What about 'em?'

'You said they're sittin' in a warehouse. You know where?'

'No.'

'Then let's find out.' Chigorin chose that moment to drop a hand to Hootie's shoulder. His wide grin split his face in half. 'I don't know about you, Hootie,' he explained, 'but I feel like a new man.'

Hootie slides into the passenger seat and shakes the cop's hand. Chigorin's drinking less these days, but his appearance hasn't changed. The cheap suit, the cheaper tie, the scuffed shoes, the bull neck, the crew cut. Retired or not, the cop looks like a cop.

'Judson, my boy,' Chigorin says, 'how ya feelin' this morning?'

'Never better.' Hootie lays the storyboard on the back seat next to a boxed Cookinart, one of six prototypes manufactured to exacting standards. These suckers actually work.

They're on their way to the studio/offices of Marty Martinez in Great Neck, a Long Island town just across the city border. After two decades in the advertising world, Martinez had opened his own studio, Inez Productions, in 2004. Cheap commercials designed to sell marginal products are Marty's specialty and he was entirely reassuring over the phone.

'Don't worry about a thing,' he told Hootie. 'I've got it under control.'

Just as well, because Chigorin and Hootie have already purchased seven thousand Cookinarts and there's no backing out now. They have to choose a studio and soon, before warehousing costs eat into their marketing budget.

'I spoke to Nick Campo last night,' Chigorin says.

Campo, the detective who inherited Bubba's case, located the homeless man Chigorin first interviewed within a few days. His name was Leonard White and he picked Bubba out of a photo array and a subsequent line-up. When that didn't satisfy the prosecutors, Campo dug up two more witnesses, both of whom saw Bubba kill the rat in the subway station, and an informant willing to swear that Bubba and the victim knew each other.

'What'd Campo have to say?'

'Bubba's gonna plead guilty to second degree murder. In return, he gets the minimum sentence, fifteen to life, and the state won't file extortion charges. But the main thing is that he's not talkin'.'

Hootie nods, but doesn't respond. The task force working the Bayside homicides connected him to Bubba early on, as he knew they would. When they asked to question him, as he also knew they would, he hadn't resisted. That's because a refusal, as Chigorin explained, would only excite their interest. But he'd stuck with the story he originally told Chigorin. He met Bubba for the first time on the subway platform and Bubba offered him a place to stay. There was nothing not to like.

Only a week before his interview with the task force, Hootie had visited Bubba on Rikers Island. By then, of course, Bubba knew that Hootie would testify against him. Hootie was there to tell Bubba that he had nothing to do with Amelia's death, but he never got the words out.

Bubba was seated behind a Plexiglas partition when Hootie pulled up. He seemed even bigger than Hootie remembered, and far more threatening. The huge skull, small features and marble-hard eyes might have been cast in stone. For a long moment he stared at Hootie through the greasy partition, a stranger gauging another stranger's intentions. Then he lifted a telephone receiver to his mouth.

'Sooner or later, they're gonna let me out,' he told Hootie. 'And when they do, I'm gonna kill ya.'

But Hootie wasn't intimidated. In fact, he'd smiled, though he never doubted Bubba's sincerity. One more thing to worry about? So fuckin' what? And by the way, thanks for the warning.

'Judson,' Chigorin says, 'you still with us?'

'Was I spacin' out again?'

'Don't worry, it's natural, given everything that happened.'

'Then what about you, Pete? You're not having any problems I can see.'

Chigorin laughs. 'Ya know, I was so sure that she was gonna kill me, it was like I was already dead. Call me Lazarus.'

Hootie echoes the cop's laughter. 'And what does that make me? Because I'm telling ya, Pete, when I look back on what happened, I don't ask myself what would Jesus do.'

'Why not? Jesus protects the innocent. I mean, I risked my career to save Amelia's ass and now she's gonna shoot me? No, you did the right thing, and when your time for judgment comes, you'll be able to defend yourself.' Chigorin pulls the car to a stop at a traffic light. They're on Northern Boulevard, heading east. 'Look, we have a little spare time. Whatta ya say we stop for breakfast? There's a diner a couple of miles up, they bake their own muffins.'

'Sounds good to me.'

Hootie glances into the back seat, at the storybook and the Cookinart. He tells himself that it's time to focus, that choosing the right studio is vital, since they don't have the money to remake the commercial. Still, Hootie's thoughts remain focused on Bubba Yablonsky just long enough for him to concede that Bubba was absolutely right about one thing.

Every great fortune begins with a crime.